SERVANTS, MASTERS *and* ROGUES

Also by Tim Davidson

The Girl from Milan

The lives of a Bristol antique clock restorer and a beautiful researcher cross paths at the grave of a long-dead British Army officer with a familiar name. His curiosity piqued, Alec 'Tick-Tock' Fraser joins a quest with Silvia on behalf of a wealthy Italian Count involving a roguish English baronet, a trip to New York and a priceless cello, all to unravel a mystery – what happened to the girl from Milan?

Time for a Party

A chance find in a village bookshop recalls an unspoken family history and propels Geoff Mumford into a world of wealth, intrigue and promiscuity. Visiting the South of France Geoff finds himself enmeshed in the story of his glamorous forbear, only for the family history to be stolen in mysterious circumstances.

Out of A Pale Blue Sky

William Wilkins is a history teacher at a minor public school in Gloucestershire and only son of a successful art dealer. Life in this quiet educational backwater is pleasant and easy-going, ideally suited to William's unadventurous nature. His agreeable life and future prospects, however, are suddenly overturned by a series of events coming without warning out of the blue. Just as William's fortunes appear to be at their lowest ebb, some surprising twists and turns occur setting his life on the road to recovery.

Time for Another?

George, Tom, Desmond and the Colonel share many a companionable drink in the Back Bar of the Sloop Inn. There, they delight in good company and a racy story – often told by one of the many visitors to this gem of the Devon coast – tales of love, infatuation, pretence and deception, of naivety, betrayal and triumph. So often entertained by stories about other folk, the four friends, however, unexpectedly find themselves the protagonists in a story of their own.

SERVANTS, MASTERS
and ROGUES

Tim Davidson

This edition published in 2025 by Stephen Morris
www.stephen-morris.co.uk

© Tim Davidson
cover illustration ©Ceren Kara

ISBN 978 1 0683039 2 0

British Library Cataloguing-in-Publication Data
A catalogue record for this book is available from
the British Library

Contents

For my wife Maddalena

Introduction

An interesting little fact drawn from musical history provided the inspiration for this book, namely that Mozart had started to write a German opera based on a famous Italian comic play The Servant of Two Masters by Carlo Goldoni. In a letter written by Mozart to his father, dated 5th February 1783, he says:

> …I am now writing a German opera for myself – I have chosen for it this play from Goldoni – Il Servitore di due Padroni – and the first act has already been translated entirely…and it is all a secret until everything is finished.

Beyond that, this book is a work of fiction. The characters and storylines (save of course for known musical and historical figures and events) are entirely fictitious. Any similarity between the names of these characters and the names of any persons (alive or dead) or between the fictional events described and real events is unintended and purely coincidental, and the same applies in respect of the names of businesses or organizations invented by the author.

This is a new edition of my book *The Bloomsbury Manuscript*, first published in 2013, fully revised and re-titled.

Tim Davidson

No man can serve two masters
Matthew 6:24

Servants, Masters *and* Rogues

Thursday 15th July 2004

"Man cannot live by silk shirts alone, Archie, dear boy," Hugo Belcher declared. "Cash's a bit short as usual. What I need is a very rich woman, someone to love and cherish me as I deserve and to pay for my holidays in Tuscany."

Hugo's income as a freelance journalist and music critic was not nearly enough to support the sort of lifestyle to which, as the man of wit and refinement he considered himself to be, he felt instinctively entitled. In fact, it was sometimes barely sufficient to cover the mortgage instalments on his flat and his monthly credit card bills. Indeed, there being no rich woman in the frame at present, he was rather depending on his old school friend Archie Kendall to pick up the bill for dinner… especially as they'd both ordered the menu gourmand, which certainly didn't come cheap at Chez Véronique, an ultra-chic restaurant in South Kensington, where they were dining that evening. After all, dear old Archie was a partner in a city firm of accountants. He could afford it.

"You could try getting a regular job, Hugo, like everyone else," Archie responded, a little tartly for such a mild-mannered man.

"Out of the question! I'm not like everyone else."

Archie raised a hand in response to a wave from some people sitting at the bar, a young woman and an older man.

"Who are they?" Hugo asked inquisitively.

"No-one you'd know… but talking of rich women, you need look no further than that one at the bar."

"Really? Tell me more."

"Well, her name's Lisa Belcanto…"

"And the miserable-looking bloke she's with who looks like a provincial undertaker?"

"Oh, he's a pension consultant, deals with Lisa's plan. I forget his name."

"So, what about this Lisa then? Quite pretty, I suppose, in a mousy sort of way."

"Petite might be a kinder word… Lisa is the daughter of Frank Belcanto. Frank is the Chairman and Chief Executive of Belcanto Continental."

"Belcanto Continental?"

"Belcanto supplies an extensive range of wine and food products to shops, stores, restaurants and hotels. Frank, or Franco as I suppose he must have been originally, came here as a boy from Sicily with his parents. His father started a small business in Manchester importing wine and olive oil from Italy which Frank inherited and expanded into the large import and distribution business it has now become. Originally, it was limited to the Manchester area where the company still has its headquarters, but now they trade nationwide. They import not only from Italy, but also now food and wine from all over Europe. Along the way, Belcanto have acquired several other businesses too. They own a chain of delis, a food packaging firm, and a major cold storage and haulage business. It's become quite a business empire. Of course, there are a few institutional investors, but Frank is still the majority shareholder. Lisa was born to his first wife, who died when she was a baby. She's Frank's only child and he's lavished riches on her, not least a substantial shareholding in the company. She's an extremely wealthy young woman."

"How very, very interesting, but I've no intention of running up and down to Manchester, even to chase a rich young woman –

unless she was a lot prettier than that one!"

"You expect too much, Hugo! Looks aren't everything. Lisa is a charming, sweet-natured young lady, and in fact she lives in London. Papa got her a job with the PR consultancy firm which advises the group on its marketing and promotional activities."

"But how do you know about all this? What's your connection?"

"My firm acts as auditors to the Belcanto Continental Group."

"I see, you wouldn't just happen to have the phone number on you of this PR outfit Lisa works for, would you, old chap?"

"You're not really serious, are you, surely?"

"Well why not? Nothing ventured, nothing gained, as the saying goes."

"Well, yes, as a matter of fact I have," Archie said, scrolling through the contact list on his mobile. "Here you are. Now look, I'm not really supposed to give out information about clients you know – professional confidentiality and all that. But what are you going to say to the girl, you're a complete stranger to her? You must promise me to be discreet."

"Don't worry, Archie, I'll think of something and I promise to be discreet." Hugo said, copying down the number.

"That'll cost you dinner, Hugo…"

"Well, next time perhaps, Archie. But in the meantime, why not come for drinks at my flat on Saturday? I'm having a few of my press friends round. Quite amusing people, some of them. There'll be the usual nibbles and some half decent champagne…"

"Sorry. Can't make it on Saturday. I'm going out with Lillian."

"Lillian? Who's Lillian? You never told me about any Lillian."

"Lillian's a new member of my Audit team."

"Oh, I see. Exercising the old droit de seigneur, eh?"

"Rubbish! We share an interest in the arts. Lillian is a very cultured young woman."

"So was Madame Pompadour."

"I'll ignore that remark. In any event, Lillian and I are going to the theatre together to see some eighteenth-century Italian comedy called… let me think… The Servant of Two Masters."

"Ah, by Goldoni?"

"Yes, I believe so. Why, do you know it?"

"Yes, it's probably Goldoni's most famous play. As a matter of fact, I went to see it a few years ago myself at the Teatro Goldoni itself, the last time I was in Venice – in Italian, mark you! It was really most entertaining."

Archie was about to joke that Hugo was himself the servant of two masters: Laziness and Self-indulgence, but thought better of it. There was, though, a grain or two of truth in it, he thought to himself with a smile.

"Good" He said instead "Something to look forward to then. Now going back to where we were… the long and short of it is that I've got to pay for your dinner yet again tonight, have I?"

"'Fraid so, Archie. But come on, old boy, you can afford it. You city types are rich beyond the dreams of avarice!"

Wednesday 1st August 1798

"But England is a far-off place of which we know little." Magdalena Malinska said, turning to face her young lover. "Oh, why must you go there, Antonin?"

It was the first day of August 1798; the same day, it so happened, as the great naval engagement known as the Battle of the Nile, though it was not at Aboukir Bay, off the coast of Egypt, where the battle was fought and Nelson won his famous victory over the French fleet, but it was far away to the north in a fine old house in a wealthy quarter of Prague where Magdalena posed her despairing question, quite oblivious to the remorseless march of history.

Antonin Vasylicek raised himself up on his elbow and making a sound, half yawn half sigh, looked down at Magdalena as she lay beside him on the bed, her head slightly tilted to one side in a mildly mocking gesture of enquiry.

"My dear Magdalena, you know why I must go. I have explained a thousand times. I must find a position worthy of the talents which God has graciously seen fit to bestow upon me. Pleasant as my duties here undoubtedly have been…"

"Is that all our love means to you then? A pleasant duty to perform when my husband happens to be away from the house, at a meeting of the Freemasons or the Guild of Goldsmiths?"

"Of course not. You tease me as always. You know very well I refer to my official duty instructing your dear daughter Marenka in the art of the fortepiano – a pleasure indeed to instruct one already so gifted – but surely you must see that I cannot forever remain a humble music teacher. I have an uncle in England, himself a respected musician, who is well connected there, and he has promised to help me establish a career as a pianist and composer. There are good prospects in England for an ambitious musician, following in the footsteps of the great Joseph Haydn…"

"A pox upon your uncle and all his promises, upon England and all her prospects and on Haydn's feet too! I want you; I need you; I love you… And what of poor Marenka? She needs your instruction and encouragement. Just as her own talents begin to blossom, her teacher deserts her. And me."

As soon as she had spoken these words, Magdalena pouted in a provocative manner that would under normal circumstances have reduced any man to putty in her hands, but Antonin was by now well used to these little ploys. His putty had long since hardened and his sang remained froid.

"But before you know it, my Sweetest Love, I shall return – and return, you may be certain, a renowned composer with a wealth of symphonies, concertos and operas to my credit, a new maestro for a new century! Marenka will be my sole pupil, my protégée, I promise. Meanwhile, Herr Dusselmayr will prove, I'm sure, a more than able teacher."

"Nonsense! Dusselmayr comes from some small provincial village, where I believe his father was the local schoolmaster. He's a simpleton, a clod of a local church organist. I cannot understand why my husband has retained him."

"Haydn too was born in a village, where his father was, if I recall correctly, a wheelwright."

"You're incorrigible, Antonin. Oh, whatever shall I do without you? But, of course, you don't really love me, do you? How else could you leave me like this?"

"Magdalena, I love you with a fervour and passion unmatched even by Eros himself, my forever-beloved…"

"Forever-beloved, indeed! You forget I know you too well, Antonin. The instant you arrive in London, you are sure to attract a bevy of pretty young English girls, all wide blue eyes, winsome smiles, and little turned-up noses. Doubtless you will pick the best of them, and, knowing your devilish good fortune, the one with the plumpest of bosoms and the wealthiest of papas – and that will be the last I hear of you!"

"My dear Magdalena, you judge me too harshly."

"Accurately enough, I think. But I have something for you… a parting gift."

"I'm intrigued. What is this something, my dearest? Let me see."

"Patience! I will fetch it for you now. I have it in my dressing room." With this, Magdalena eased herself off the bed and, stooping to retrieve her nightgown from the floor to cover her nakedness, glided towards the door which led to the small anteroom adjoining the bedchamber.

Antonin watched her go, marvelling as always at the extraordinary grace with which she performed even the simplest of tasks. As she disappeared next door, he lay back once more on the bed, raising his eyes to admire the elaborate rococo plaster-work weaving its intricate patterns across the ceiling. Dreamily he recalled the warm summer evening in July 1796, over two years before, when he had first entered the imposing house near St Thomas's Church which had been the Malinska family home for more than a century. He had been engaged, along with two other local musicians, to play in a trio at a soirée to celebrate Josef and Magdalena's wedding anniversary.

Josef Malinska, a prosperous city merchant, was rather older than his wife, Magdalena. A large, gruff, slightly austere figure, much absorbed in his work and the performance of his civic duties, he often seemed ill at ease in the company of his beautiful, vivacious spouse and her circle of witty, cultured friends. It was not perhaps altogether surprising that she had developed a taste for younger men.

Antonin's urbane manner belied his age. He was only twenty-four years old when he first met Magdalena and she was almost old enough to be his mother. Just as she liked younger men, Antonin had a penchant for older women – along, that is, with his penchant for their nubile daughters and not to mention his equally enthusiastic penchant for pretty young housemaids. There was something, though, especially alluring about Magdalena, apart from her obvious physical attributes. If he could only succeed in seducing her it would be a triumph to end all triumphs. Her beauty was famed throughout Prague, and there would be the added piquancy of making a cuckold out of one of the city's wealthiest and most influential citizens. In any case, Josef was a monstrous old bore who certainly didn't deserve to keep such a rare creature as Magdalena all to himself.

Aware of his lowly status as a paid performer, Antonin thought that he would have little opportunity to speak with Magdalena that evening, but several times, as he played, he caught her casting him a quick glance and then almost as quickly looking away again. It was to him, experienced in these matters as he was, despite his youth, a quite unmistakable sign. After the music had finished and the evening drew to a close, she moved near enough for him to manage to address a few words to her. He wasted no time in exerting the full force of his exceptionally beguiling charm. If there had been such a thing as a Guild of Charmers in Prague, Antonin would surely have been elected its Master and not a vote against.

Two days after the evening of the soirée, a note arrived at his lodgings, delivered by Magdalena's maid, summoning him again to the Malinska household. He was shown into the music room in which he had recently performed and where Magdalena herself was waiting to receive him. She complimented him extravagantly on 'the exceptional sensitivity of his playing' and implored him to accept an appointment as her daughter's music teacher. Flattered, Antonin had hastened to agree. He sensed, though, during the course of the interview, that there was something else about Magdalena's manner and tone of voice, something too subtle to define, something implicit in the way in which she referred to his sensitivity which led him to believe that there was more to her proposal than the mere instruction of her daughter in the art of playing the fortepiano.

And so there was! Towards the end of Marenka's second lesson, Magdalena appeared in the music room to ask Antonin if he might spare her a few moments in the library before he took his leave.

It is perhaps a paradox that in all the great poetic literature of the world more lines have probably been penned in celebration of passion, love and romance than upon any other theme, yet when it comes to the crucial moment in these matters words are so often superfluous, an embarrassment even. Thus, it was that as the library door closed behind them, Antonin and Magdalena fell at once into each other's arms and their lips met before a word had passed between them, other than "Oh, My Darling Magdalena" and "Come to me now, you gorgeous young scoundrel". It was to be the prelude to a long, amorous adventure.

Though some aspiring musicians did indeed sometimes leave Prague to take up positions elsewhere at some stately German or Bohemian court, Antonin had no particular wish to desert his native city. However, his personal circumstances were such that he felt it only prudent to depart; and depart, moreover, in some haste and for a destination as far away as possible. His taste for fine clothes and high living had led him to incur a veritable burden of debt … a chain of liabilities from which it would be nigh impossible now to disentangle himself, reliant only as he was on his meagre earnings as a music teacher.

Antonin always left the house immediately after Marenka's music lesson, and Magdalena would arrange for her trusty maid to slip a note to him, as he made his exit, advising him of a suitable time when Josef would be absent and thus when it would be safe for him to return. In the interests of discretion, he would re-enter the house, just as he had that evening, by a door at the rear used by tradesmen, to which Magdalena had provided him the key. The trouble was that Gladic, Josef's sour-faced secretary, harboured suspicions. Of this Antonin was quite certain from the way Gladic looked at him whenever they met – the narrowing of the eyes, the sly nod, the knowing smirk. Once, indeed, he had run into him in the rear alleyway just after he had left the house, and he was sure the wretched fellow was keeping watch. How long would it be before his suspicions were confirmed and the game was up?

Nor was this the only matter of some delicacy in his life. There were, too, his dalliances with the pretty young wife of a banker and with the daughter of a city magistrate. The banker's wife was threatening suicide unless he promised to elope with her and the magistrate's daughter had just tearfully informed him that she suspected herself to be with child – his child.

At any moment, Antonin feared, he would be pursued through the streets of Prague by a cohort of murderous husbands and outraged fathers out for his blood, not to mention a further cohort of angry creditors after their money. He would be very lucky if his body were not found floating one day soon in the swirling waters of the River Vltava unless he urgently made good his escape.

His Uncle Jan in London had not in fact made any promises to help him at all. Indeed, they had not corresponded in years and Antonin doubted very much whether he had any influence with anyone in England of any rank or importance whatever. The last news he had received was that Jan had forsaken his musical career as a flautist to become the landlord of an alehouse. England, however, seemed a suitably far off place to go where he might be safe from the perils which now threatened to engulf him.

Interrupting these unpleasant reflections as they flashed through his mind, Magdalena returned bearing what appeared to be a bulky manuscript of some sort.

"Here you are, my darling Antonin. This is for you."

"But what is it, my love?"

"It's the score and libretto of an opera…a German opera though taken from a well-known Italian play. Josef found it in a chest in that old house of his by the Charles Bridge. You know the one he lets out. It must have been left behind by one of his tenants. I have no use for it, of course, but I thought you might like it. It says in the score it's by Herr Mozart, by the way, but I hardly think that likely. Here, take it."

Antonin sat up in bed to take it from her as she thrust it

towards him.

Looking at the first page of the score, Antonin read slowly out loud the title of the work which was written rather grandly in a large but neat hand at the top of the page: "Der Diener Zweier Herren." After a brief pause, he repeated the title but this time in his own Czech tongue: "The Servant of Two Masters." Then he read the words inscribed beneath, translating from the German as he went: "A comic opera in three acts by Wolfgang Amadeus Mozart after a play by Carlo Goldoni."

"An appropriate title, is it not?"

"Appropriate?"

"Are you not yourself the servant of two masters, Antonin?"

"How do you mean? You're talking in riddles, my darling. What masters are these?"

"Love and Music, of course. But no man, as we know, can be a servant of two masters, and you have chosen to forsake me to pursue your musical ambitions."

Antonin was indeed the servant of two masters, but not precisely those which Magdalena had mentioned; Antonin's two masters had always been Pleasure and Self-preservation and it was true that the dictates of the one were sometimes in conflict with the requirements of the other. At present the latter held sway, but he hoped to resume employment with the former as soon as he was safely in England. As adept as he was at feigning sincerity, Antonin could not quite bring himself to look Magdalena full in the eye.

"On the contrary, my life is dedicated above all else to love, my love for you, my dearest." He managed to say, "Like some lovesick soldier campaigning in a distant land who longs for a swift victory and a safe return to his beloved," He continued, warming to the task, "so shall I yearn for the day when my musical conquests are won and I may return to take you in my arms!"

"A pretty speech, Antonin. If only it were true!"

"But it is true, every word!" Antonin protested, swiftly looking away, and pretending to study the opera score.

"Well, there's no call to look at that now, Antonin! Plenty of time for that later, on your travels. Now is the time for another concerto!" she said, throwing off her gown and mounting the bed beside him. "Let us begin with a short fiery allegro with a rousing entry by the soloist, next a long lingering adagio, and then of course the final rondo… molto vivace!"

Casting aside the manuscript on the dumpy Flemish commode beside the bed, Antonin prepared himself for yet another virtuoso performance.

Friday 16th July 2004

"Louther and Tomkins, may I help you?"

"Yes, I wonder if I could speak to Miss Belcanto?"

"I'll put you through. Please hold the line."

"Hello. Lisa Belcanto speaking."

"Hello, Miss Belcanto. My name is Hugo Belcher. You won't know me, but I'm a journalist researching an article for *The Economist* on women in business," Hugo lied fluently. "I appreciate this comes quite out of the blue but I wonder if you might consider granting me the favour of an interview?"

"You sure you don't want my line manager, Dorothy Cleaver? I mean she's been working here for ages and she sits on some important committee appointed by the government about getting more women into senior management jobs, female equality issues, that sort of thing…"

"No, no, Lisa – may I call you Lisa? Sorry, I don't mean to be presumptuous."

"Of course." Lisa very much liked the sound of his posh velvety accent. It made her come over in goose pimples. She couldn't help herself.

"The fact is," Hugo continued, "that I really want to hear things from the perspective of the younger generation, as it were – especially the views and experiences of a clever young woman such as yourself."

"I see, but… but… how did you get hold of my name?"

"Oh, we journalists have our sources, you know, and your name came up as just the right sort of person for my purposes. I mean, for this interview."

Hugo had been about to mention Frank Belcanto, but thought better of it. He didn't want Lisa to think that his only interest in her was because of whose daughter she was.

"I see," Lisa said, feeling quite flattered. "Well, I suppose there could be no harm in it…"

"I'll take that as a yes then, if that's all right. Now, may I be permitted to take you out for dinner? It's the very least I can do in return for your help and I'm sure it would make for a more relaxed setting for our interview. Do you think that would be a good idea?"

"Thank you. That would be very nice, yes."

"Good, good. May I suggest a little place, a favourite of mine actually, called Chez Véronique in South Kensington, not far from the tube station?" Hugo continued, airily dismissing the fact that he could barely afford dinner for one at Chez Véronique, let alone two. Too bad – it would all just have to go on his much-abused credit card. "Do you know it by any chance?"

"Yes, I do, it's a favourite of mine, too!"

"Really? What a coincidence! When did you last go there, if I may ask?"

"Yesterday."

"Good heavens, how extraordinary! I was there yesterday

myself. Now let me guess… You weren't by any chance the girl in the smart blue trouser suit, with long dark brown hair… accompanied, if I recall correctly, by a tall distinguished-looking gentleman wearing glasses?"

"Well, I was wearing my blue trouser suit, yes… and Derek Waltham, the man I was with, is certainly tall and distinguished, but how… how did you know? The place was full of all sorts of people. Just about any of them could have been me."

"I have a natural intuition for these things. I can picture people from the way they sound when they speak… particularly, I have to say, when it comes to attractive young ladies."

"Ooh! Ooh! I mean, how amazing!"

Lisa's mind was in turmoil. Should she really accept an invitation to go out to dinner with a complete stranger? On the other hand, this Hugo sounded just the posh, sophisticated type of man that she had been dying to meet ever since she came to London. Most of the other girls in the office seemed to have posh boyfriends, but they were mostly very posh themselves. Lisa, though her father had sent her to a good school, was painfully aware that she didn't come from quite the same sort of background as they did. Perhaps having a really posh boyfriend might even things up, enabling her to join the charmed circle of posh people to which she so aspired to belong… Perhaps, Lisa thought, letting her hopes run away with her, Hugo might be the one, the answer to her prayers.

"Would a week today, that's next Friday the 23rd, be convenient for you?"

"That would be fine." Any day of course would have been convenient for Lisa. She would have cancelled any engagement to meet Hugo.

"Excellent. I suggest I pick you up from your home in a cab at about eight. Would that be all right?"

"Oh yes, that would be wonderful. Thank you. I live at 6A Wellington Mews West. It's just off Bayswater Road, not far from Lancaster Gate."

"Yes, I think I know where you mean. I look forward to meeting you, Lisa. Something tells me that we are going to get along very well together, very well indeed. I just have an instinct for these things, you know."

Poor Lisa. Little did she realise, but Hugo's silky telephone manner was but an amuse-bouche before the full menu gourmand of charm to which she would soon be subjected…

Tuesday 11th September 1798

"Fine sweet oranges, fine lemons!"

"Flowers, fresh flowers, penny a bunch!"

"Hot spiced gingerbread!"

Antonin awoke to the cries of the street vendors in the broad thoroughfare overlooked by the coaching inn in which he had passed his first night in London. He must seek out his Uncle Jan, he thought, as he wiped the sleep from his eyes. It was not that he had any particular desire to visit his uncle or any sense of family duty which impelled him to do so. It was simply a case of empty pockets. He had all but spent the money with which he had started out from Prague including the not inconsiderable sum which Magdalena, struggling to hold back her tears, had generously thrust into his hands as he took his leave of her.

The inn where he was staying was not too far from St. Paul's Cathedral, and he believed that his uncle's tavern was somewhere in the vicinity and was known as something with the word 'Bell' or 'Bells' in its name.

He dimly recalled his father reading out a letter from Uncle Jan to this effect. His parents had passed away some years ago, but his old Aunt Sofia was still alive. How he wished now that he'd had the presence of mind to speak to her before he left Prague to ascertain if she had any better information. *Fool, fool that I am,* he chided himself. What if his uncle had moved on elsewhere in London or to another town in England or taken ship to the new world or worse still, had made his final voyage to the next one? True, Uncle Jan was younger than his father but he must surely be sixty if he was a day.

Antonin was not one to be down-hearted for long, though, even when the circumstances gave no great cause for optimism. Soon recovering his spirits and fortified by an excellent breakfast, he set forth in the direction of St. Paul's. At least Wren's great masterpiece would not itself be difficult to find. It towered above the London skyline. If ever it was temporarily lost to sight, it soon loomed up again in all its massive baroque splendour.

Before long Antonin was exploring the narrow streets and lanes around the cathedral, and almost at once found himself opposite an inn promisingly called 'The Ring of Bells'. But the innkeeper was one Jack Finch, and nobody had heard of Jan Vasylicek. Antonin made an effort to enquire of Mr Finch whether he knew of any other inn or tavern in the neighbourhood with 'Bell' in its name, but his limited English was not up to the task. Mr Finch clearly thought that Antonin was some type of troublemaker, possibly even one of those foreign revolutionaries, and promptly marched him off the premises. A little disappointed, Antonin retraced his steps and set off again in another direction.

Nearly two hours passed with no luck. He had stopped passers-by in the street to ask. "Bell, bells?" he pleaded.

All he got in response was laughter at best or, more often, blank or hostile stares. People thought him drunk or deranged. It was infuriating not to be able to explain himself properly.

London, or at least this part of it, seemed awash with taverns:

The Prince of Denmark, The White Horse, The Black Horse, The Sword and Scimitar, The Angel, The Monkey's Paw… but no other establishment, it seemed, with 'Bell' in its name. A trifle weary and frustrated, he entered a hostelry called The Green Man, and somehow, with much gesticulating, managed to order himself a pint of ale. It proved to be utterly disgusting. He could barely bring himself to finish it. Was this place, Antonin thought, called The Green Man because its patrons turned green when they drank its ale? What a waste of his slender resources!

Not in the least refreshed, as he had hoped, he left The Green Man to continue his wanderings, and there right on the opposite side of the street, tucked away in its own little courtyard only a few steps away, was another tavern which he had failed before to notice. It was called 'The Bell and Candle'.

There were a number of patrons to whom a jolly buxom girl was serving food. Antonin asked after Jan Vasylicek, but the landlord's name was John Vascoe and he was out collecting provisions or so Antonin understood.

Disconsolately, he sat down at the nearest unoccupied table.

The jolly buxom girl moved around the crowded room, squeezing her pleasingly ample figure between tables, giggling loudly and engaging patrons in rude banter as she went. Her bubbly demeanour was infectious and Antonin's doleful mood soon evaporated like a morning mist with the warmth of the rising sun.

Eventually she reached Antonin's table.

"Do you wish for something to eat, stranger?" she enquired, miming the act of eating.

"Yes, yes, I like," he said, with a suggestive wink and a grin.

Just at this moment the door swung open, and a big red-faced man entered, bearing a large basket.

"Mary, take this to the back kitchen, will you?" he called out.

Antonin looked up at the big man whom he presumed to be the landlord. Fifteen years might have passed since they had last met, back when he was a boy, but there was absolutely no doubt about it. The big red-faced man was without a doubt his uncle Jan Vasylicek, no matter that he now chose to call himself John Vascoe. As he passed the table where he was seated, Antonin leapt to his feet.

"Greetings, Uncle Jan!" he said in his native language. "I hope I find you in good health."

Jan looked back at him in blank astonishment for some seconds, his mouth agape, until his old red face crinkled in a broad smile.

"Why it's little Antonin, isn't it?" he responded, also in Czech. "I can scarcely believe it… But, but what on earth are you doing here in London?"

"I came to further my musical career."

"Your musical career?!"

"Yes."

"And had you no other reason for leaving your hearth and home?"

"Well… um… it is true that various circumstances made it desirable for me to leave Prague."

"Ah circumstances! I guessed there might be. By circumstances, I expect you mean you were in debt and your creditors were pressing for the long overdue return of their money, eh?"

"Well, I did owe some… some trifling amounts, yes."

"Anything else? Some embarrassment over a woman, perhaps?"

"Women, actually, if you must know, uncle," Antonin replied, resigning himself to the truth. This was uncanny, but there had never been any keeping secrets from his old Uncle Jan. He just seemed to know everything. If Antonin wanted his help, he reckoned, he'd better keep his answers true.

"I knew it! Much the same reasons that brought me here too – insolvency, adultery, poltroonery of every kind. Good boy! It's nice to know that you're preserving our great family traditions. I'm proud of you, though I doubt if your father would have been."

"My father was a good and honest man!"

"Precisely. Indeed, he was. But he was the white sheep of the family… the only one. I put it down to his marrying your mother, a truly virtuous woman. May God save us from virtuous women! Now, Antonin, my boy, you haven't sought out your old uncle for simple amusement or duty's sake, I'm quite sure. I suppose you're penniless and in need of a roof over your head. Well, there is a small attic room here where you are welcome to stay, if you so wish. I imagine you have left some baggage and personal belongings wherever it was you stayed last night. I will send someone with a cart to fetch them for you."

"Thank you, uncle. I shall be forever in your debt."

"And a lot of good that will do me!" Uncle Jan said with a knowing smile.

Some hours later, Antonin sat in the taproom at The Bell and Candle. It was full that evening and the clientele was a varied one. There were huddles of prosperous-looking, well-attired traders and merchants earnestly talking about the business of the day, a gaggle of young apprentices from a nearby printers' workshop, a brace of worldly-wise lawyers' clerks, and a fair collection of Thames lightermen, cobblers and persons of that ilk. There were some rougher characters too of the sort that one would certainly not wish to meet in a dark alley at night, not unless you were prepared to risk being unburdened of the contents of your pockets or worse.

It struck Antonin that The Bell and Candle reflected on a tiny scale his initial impression of England's great capital city, the little he had seen of it – a city where fine houses and graceful churches jostled with taverns, gin shops and brothels; a vast, growing city where great wealth and elegance neighboured poverty, crime, drunkenness and squalor; a city of high spirits, low morals and a whiff of danger.

Antonin was not alone for long but soon found himself joined by three young women, Ella, Josie and Grace. Grace stood leaning over him from behind, her arms round his neck, Josie sat on his knee and Ella sat opposite him at the table staring into his eyes. Magdalena Malinska had foreseen that a bevy of young English girls would descend upon him as soon as he arrived in England and that he would choose one with a plump bosom and a wealthy papa, a choice which would ensure for him a life of idle pleasure thereafter. These three were not, however, quite the bevy of young English girls that Magdalena would have had in mind. Though Ella, the blonde of the trio, certainly had a deep enough cleavage, none of them, he felt quite sure, could boast a wealthy papa.

Ella, Josie and Grace were, of course, no more than common whores simply looking to ply their trade. They had fixed their attentions on Antonin because he seemed like a good prospect for business, being a well-dressed young man with a splendid waistcoat and expensive boots. He was very handsome, too, which made a pleasant change from most of their clients.

"What be thy name, stranger?" Ella asked.

"Antonin."

"Odd name… foreign, I'll wager."

"Yes. I come many miles… from Prague."

"Never 'eard of it. Be thee a Frenchie?" Grace asked.

"Course 'e's not French, you foolish tart!" Josie laughed.

"And see who calls me a tart, then !" Grace rejoined.

Ignoring Grace and Josie, Ella leant forward over the table, bringing her face very close to Antonin's and staring ever more intently into his eyes.

"I'm yours for a shilling, stranger, seeing you be so young and handsome," she whispered.

At this point, a man at the next table turned his head to address Antonin directly.

"If you take my advice, sir, you'll do well to withhold your custom from that little profligate. The last time I took my pleasure of her, she left me with a severe dose of Cupid's revenge – a fine reward for my patronage!"

Ella let fly with a stream of expletives.

"And how would you know? A man who's dipped his engine into every harlot between here and the Haymarket, even those flea-ridden hags in Covent Garden, I shouldn't wonder!"

Antonin was quite at a loss to understand these exchanges, but smiled charmingly nonetheless. He had no illusions, though, as to the sort of women Ella, Grace and Josie were, and though he enjoyed their company, he had never once paid for pleasure with a woman and was not about to change his habits now. Besides, in his present tenuous financial condition a shilling was a precious sum which he was in no position to fritter away on idle pleasure. The three tarts, realising that they were pursuing a lost cause, finally moved off, leaving him in peace to enjoy the simple but filling supper which jolly buxom Mary placed in front of him.

As the evening wore on, the tavern became fuller, the ale flowed in ever greater quantities, and its patrons, raising their tankards, became ever louder and their voices slurred. The respectable folk had left for their homes to be replaced by an increasing number of local revellers. Antonin decided it was time for bed. He wished goodnight to his uncle who thrust a candle into his hand. Slowly he clambered his way up the long, steep, winding stairway to the garret at the top of the building. It was very dark, too, and just as well that he had something to light his way.

Finally, with a grateful sigh, he reached the small room his uncle had allotted him and made his way towards the bed, placing the candle in its holder on the table beside it. The trunk with his belongings lay on the floor nearby, still half-unpacked. Looking down on it he noticed, peeping out from beneath a pile of soiled shirts, the opera manuscript which Magdalena had given to him in Prague. He had not inspected it at all on his journey nor had he felt any inclination to do so. On impulse, however, he picked it up and climbed onto the bed with it.

Holding it up to the candlelight, he had just begun to peruse the music of the overture but had read no further than the opening few bars when the door creaked open and Ella appeared.

"Let us not let a shilling come between us, my dear," she said. "'Tis but a paltry sum and I happily forgo it."

The manuscript slipped from his fingers and dropped to the floor as he turned to take young Ella in his arms as she eased herself onto the bed beside him.

It would be some while before he found the time to examine the score again.

Friday 23rd July 2004

"Frobisher Design Studio, how may I help you?"

"Is that you, Sandra?"

"Yes, it's me," Sandra Grisewood answered.

"Well, it's Adam here. Look, I've managed to book somewhere this evening for your birthday treat. Sorry I can't manage a drink before, though. I've got some literary agent coming in to see me. I'll go on straight from here and we'll meet at the restaurant if that's okay."

"Where are we like going, then?"

"Do you know Chez Véronique in South Kensington?"

Well, of course Sandra knew Chez Véronique. It was London's latest hot spot for the famous, the fashionable and anyone else who could afford the eye-watering prices. Its landmark canopied entrance was often featured in glossy magazines as a backdrop to pictures of glitzy celebrities and its chef was the latest doyen of the culinary arts and already a well-known television personality in his own right.

"Oh, Adam, of course I know where it is! What a surprise!"

"Don't be silly, Sandra. I didn't mean I'd booked there… Who'd ever want to eat in a place like that patronised by all those ghastly rich and vulgar types? Besides, can you imagine the expense! No, the place I've booked is called the Oriental Temple. It's one of those Pan-Asian restaurants. John, our cashier, recommended it. He said the food's quite good and it's reasonably cheap. From the direction you'll be coming from, it's three doors down from Chez Véronique on the same side of the road. The table is booked for eight o'clock."

Typical! Sandra thought. You'd think that for her birthday, Adam might just once have booked somewhere special and blow the cost. Indeed, cost would not have been a problem if only Adam had a decently paid job… And he bloody well should have one, too. He had come down from Cambridge with a First in History. He could easily by now be a junior partner in a city law firm or a rising star at the Foreign Office or whatever, but no – he had gone on instead to work for his uncle at an old-fashioned publishing company in a dark and dingy basement in Clapham. It specialised in publishing learned works on subjects like the Rise and Fall of the Hittite kingdom, Elizabethan lute music, seventeenth-century Scandinavian poetry and things of that kind.

These were not glossy coffee table books or books designed to entice a mass readership. Neither authors nor publishers were ever likely to become owners of Tuscan castles or yachts moored in some fashionable Mediterranean marina. No, they did it simply for the love of the thing and indeed Adam truly enjoyed his job and the eclectic mix of people with whom it brought him into contact. It suited his temperament ideally. He had absolutely no worldly ambition… that was the trouble.

However, notwithstanding his unworldliness and lack of drive, Sandra loved Adam dearly, and they had been living together for nearly a year now at his small studio flat in Battersea. He was at heart, she knew, a good bloke, being kind, good-natured and humorous. He was handsome, too, in a Bohemian sort of way. She had tried to improve the way in which he dressed but he rarely wore the things she bought for him, preferring to turn out in his old cords, scuffed at the knees, and an ancient tweed sports jacket purchased at a local charity shop. It was slightly too small for him, patched at the elbows and exuded a faint whiff of stale tobacco smoke. That's what, come to think of it, he'd been wearing when he left the flat that morning and that's what he'd be wearing in the evening. Just as well, perhaps, they weren't going to Chez Véronique after all. Ah well, she sighed, oriental it would just have to be.

Sandra was quite different in temperament to Adam, a most single-minded young woman who knew exactly what she wanted. Her job working as a receptionist, secretary and general factotum for a small firm of interior designers in Chelsea was fun, but it was just a job. It was not only money she wanted – money for a bigger flat, designer clothes, holidays in Thailand and so forth, though she did crave all these things. No, Sandra wanted more than that. She wanted to be someone, and what Sandra wanted, more than anything else in the world, was to be an opera singer, a great soprano.

Becoming an opera singer was perhaps an unlikely ambition for a working-class girl from an industrial town in the north-east

Midlands, and indeed, until Mr. Peabody came on the scene, Sandra had known as much about opera as anyone not actually a marine biologist might be expected to know about the life cycle of the Sulawesi Island Hairy Frogfish.

It was Mr Peabody, the choir-master of St Gideon's, her local parish church, who had first recognised that she had a quite exceptional voice. After some years working as an office junior, she decided to attend the local technical college for a course in bookkeeping, and it was during this period that she had applied to join the choir of St. Gideon's Church. But for this, her vocal ability might have gone entirely unnoticed, though her application to join the choir was not prompted by a sudden interest in church music or a rush of religious fervour but for quite another reason.

Sandra had a problem. All the boys she knew liked to have a good time. A 'good time' of course meant lots of clubbing, drinking, sex and watching footie. The girls also liked to have a good time which meant much the same thing, with perhaps a little less emphasis on the footie. Watching footie on the big screen at the pub or going clubbing were naturally the highlights of the week.

The town's largest and rowdiest disco was situated conveniently close to the Horace Rampton Memorial Park, a small artery of scrubby greenness near the town centre named after Sir Horace Rampton, a local Victorian worthy whose invention of a small mechanical hoist had been the foundation of the town's original prosperity. His statue stood, tall and proud, in the middle of the park, and it was here, too, that young clubbers often congregated in the early hours of the morning after leaving the club and where, in the pale moonlight, they sought sexual gratification, their urges already inflamed by a heady mix of throbbing music, ecstasy and alcopops. Indeed, it was estimated that approximately one-third of the babies born to single mothers in the area were conceived beneath the stony sightless stare of good old Sir Horace in the park which bore his name.

Sandra thought that life ought to offer something rather better than this, though she didn't know quite what or where to find it. That was her problem.

The boys, whose attentions she scorned, thought that she was a silly, stuck-up little bitch, and the girls resented what they saw as her attempt to be superior. Even her loyal friend Betty told her that she was 'like missing out on things'.

In truth, Sandra was desperate to find a nice boyfriend; not one of those silly blokes at the disco, but someone who might unlock the door of that better and brighter world which she was sure must somewhere exist. Moreover, she thought that she had identified who this might be. His name was Jonathan Clitheroe. Jonathan was about four years older than she was. He had attended a private school and from there went on to university where he had obtained a degree in Chemistry. He now worked for a pharmaceutical research company which had offices and a laboratory at the small science park off the ring road on the edge of town. He was obviously brainy, Sandra thought, and really very handsome too.

Jonathan lived with his parents in the same road as Sandra, Station Road, but at the better, more fashionable end. The old station itself, near Sandra's home, was defunct and the branch line had closed down many years before. The railway tracks too had been taken up and the course of the old line was now used as a cycle track. Every day Jonathan cycled along it on his way to work. Sandra had a very good view of the track from her bedroom window. The trouble was that she had only ever spoken to Jonathan once at a fireworks party organised by the neighbourhood watch group. She knew, however, that he was a member of St. Gideon's Church choir because she had seen him singing in it at the previous year's Christmas Carol Concert, hence the reason for Sandra's application to join. She had thought of stepping out in front of his bike, pretending that she had not seen him coming, but came to the conclusion that it would be just too risky and the end result was not sufficiently predictable. Joining the choir would give her the opportunity to get to know him properly, and it would please her parents, too, who might just give her the money to go skiing with her friend Betty after Christmas. It was, she thought, a win-win situation, an expression she had heard some prancing politician use on the television. Later, maturity would teach her to be wary of political utterances of this sort, but in truth it really would turn out to be a win-win situation – though not quite in the way she had imagined.

When Mr Peabody auditioned her, he realised at once that she had a great natural talent. He had tried to tell her so but at this stage she took little notice. She was just relieved to have been accepted as a member of the choir, which would enable her to pursue her all-important mission to woo Jonathan Clitheroe.

The trouble was that Jonathan did not seem all that receptive of her advances. Sandra was nothing if not persistent, however, and eventually she managed to persuade him to take her out for a pizza one evening after choir practice.

He seemed rather nervous, and initially conversation was difficult.

"Apart from the choir, what do you like doing?" she asked him, trying to keep things neutral and unthreatening. "Do you have a special hobby?"

"Ornithology," he answered shyly.

"How interesting!" Sandra said as enthusiastically as she could, not having the faintest clue what ornithology was but not wanting to admit it.

It would not be long, however, before she found out. Encouraged by her response, Jonathan launched into a very detailed explanation of the difference between a Swallow, a Swift and a House Martin. This was before he described in even more elaborate detail the life cycle and habits of the Green Woodpecker, the Great Tit and the Sedge Warbler respectively; and of course, how the habits of the Sedge Warbler differed from those of all the other Warblers. The evening was not a roaring success.

Some while later, Sandra met Betty for a coffee at Starbucks. Betty was not her normal jolly self. There was something she wanted to say, but was clearly finding it a bit difficult to say it.

"Look, Sandra," she finally blurted out, "I got to tell you. Jonathan is like engaged… to a girl he met at university. He proposed at the weekend when they went off together to the Dales, bird-watching or something. I know 'cos my mum cleans for the Clitheroes twice a week. I'm really like sorry, Sandra, I really am."

But for Gordon Peabody, Sandra would most likely have left the choir after the Jonathan Clitheroe debacle, but he had managed to persuade her to stay. His influence on her life proved to be truly pivotal, and through him Sandra became aware that she had something special to offer the world other than a pretty face and an attractive figure. Not only did she attend the regular choir practices, but once a week Mr. Peabody kindly found time to give her some personal one-to-one coaching at his home, free of charge. He introduced her, too, to the wonders of what he referred to as 'proper music'. A wave of classical CDs, especially famous choral masterpieces and opera highlights, began to crowd the shelves in her bedroom.

The real turning point came, however, when Mr Peabody arranged to take her along with a small party of choir members to a performance of The Marriage of Figaro at Buxton. She had never been to the opera before and was totally captivated. That evening Sandra's great ambition to become an opera singer was born.

The next day, she told Mr Peabody about her dream, at which

he smiled in his usual kindly fashion. Privately, though, he thought it just a passing girlish fantasy in much the same way as little girls often dream of becoming ballet dancers after being taken to see a performance of The Nutcracker at Christmas time. Instead, he encouraged her to join the local choral society, which would have a much larger repertoire than the church choir and more opportunities for solo work.

It was not enough. Mr Peabody had reckoned without Sandra's iron determination. Her great ambition continued to simmer away on the back-burner of her mind, every now and then boiling over in a bubbling brew of hope, disappointment and frustration.

Sandra soon became disillusioned with her course in bookkeeping, frustrated with living at home with her parents, and tired of the dreary little town of her birth where nothing much of importance ever seemed to happen. Though she had only been there once on a school outing to the Houses of Parliament, she knew that London was the place for her. Of course, in the back of her mind, too, was the thought that the great metropolis might one day offer her the opportunity of realising her dream.

A former school friend, who had previously moved to London to work, offered her a temporary bed in the flat she shared with three other girls. She was lucky enough to find a good job quite quickly. The interior design studio where she worked was smart and exclusive. Sandra was employed there in the office as a secretary alongside the boss's personal assistant, Fiona. Though plainly from a very classy background, Fiona was a kind and friendly girl and took Sandra under her wing. It was she who had introduced her to Adam.

Romance blossomed and only a few months later Sandra had moved into his flat.

Poor old Albert Grisewood, Sandra's father, an electrician by trade, was furious – furious that she had abandoned her bookkeeping course, more furious still when she announced she was leaving home for London, and quite speechlessly furious when he learnt later that she had moved in with a man. The course would have given her great opportunities of advancement, not least a good job in the accounts department of Falkland Crane plc, the town's principal employer. What was she doing living with some upper-class twit in London? What was wrong with an honest local lad, for heaven's sake, if she wanted someone to walk out with? She had thrown her life away, and as for this idea of becoming an opera singer of all things – what on earth was she thinking?

Sandra's mother, June, was inclined to take a different view, though one she kept to herself. To begin with, she didn't believe, as her husband did, that Adam was just a silly young toff with whom their daughter could have absolutely nothing in common. She knew her daughter to be a very determined young woman, and thought perhaps she might make something of this singing business. After all, other girls, not necessarily from a privileged background, had famously succeeded in doing so. Everyone said Sandra had such a beautiful voice. June herself, as a young woman, had nurtured an ambition to become a doctor. Nothing had come of it of course. The nearest she had ever come to the medical profession was to be a part-time receptionist at a local GP surgery. She had married Albert in her early twenties and soon became pregnant with Sandra and that was that. It would be nice if Sandra could succeed where she had failed. She continued to hope and pray in silence.

Sandra's boss had most kindly invited her, along with Fiona, for a drink to celebrate her birthday in a local wine bar after work. This conveniently filled up the time before her rendezvous with Adam. She could easily have walked to the restaurant if she'd left the wine bar a bit earlier. It was not that far. As it was – and feeling slightly guilty about it – she took a taxi. For the fun of it, she told the cabbie she wanted to go to Chez Véronique. At least for the duration of the journey she could foster the illusion that that was where she was really going; after all, it was only three doors distant from where she was actually going, even though it was a world apart in every other sense.

Being fair to Adam this oriental place probably wouldn't be that bad, but would she ever be content with a life where everything was 'not that bad', 'reasonable', 'might have been a lot worse', a life of making the best of what comes? No, she bloody well wouldn't, though of course she'd have to put up with it for now… until her lucky break came along.

As her taxi pulled up alongside the famous portals of Chez Véronique, another taxi was disgorging its occupants onto the pavement, a man and a woman. The man, who was busy paying off the driver, was tall, well-dressed and very good-looking. The girl he was with was small and rather ordinary. Strange, Sandra thought. One would have expected a man like that to be escorting some real beauty. At least Adam had got the better of the deal, she prided herself. The man looked, on the face of it, a model of gentlemanly respectability, but there was just something about him which suggested to Sandra, ever sensitive to such things, that he was not quite all that he seemed. As she left her taxi and crossed the path of the man and his lady friend, who were heading across the pavement towards the entrance of Chez Véronique, the pashmina shawl Sandra was wearing slipped from her shoulders. The man stooped to retrieve it from the ground where it had fallen.

"Pardon me but I think you've dropped your shawl," he said, handing it back to her with a charming smile.

"Oh, thank you, thank you very much," she said.

Their eyes met for an instant. The look he gave her confirmed her suspicions. He was, for sure, a bit of a rogue, the upmarket equivalent of the leering scaffolder who had wolf-whistled at her when she passed a building site on the way to work that morning. Well, he was the wolf without the whistle, the handsome wolf in a well-cut suit, the most dangerous kind of wolf of all… a wolf with charm. In spite of herself, she experienced a sudden frisson of excitement. Quickly she turned away and walked on briskly down the street towards the Oriental Temple. Had it not been for Adam and had the man been on his own that evening, she had a feeling that their conversation might not have ended quite so abruptly. Who knows what might have happened next?

Straining to dismiss these unsettling thoughts from her head, she entered the Oriental Temple and there was dear, dependable Adam, sitting, waiting for her at the bar. One day, though, she promised herself, she would arrive at Chez Véronique, heads would turn and people would whisper, "Look, there's Sandra Grisewood, the sensational new soprano taht everyone's talking about."

Hugo Belcher and Lisa Belcanto arrived at Chez Véronique by taxi as arranged. There was a short distance to walk to reach the entrance beneath its red and blue striped awning and between the bay trees in their ornately moulded terracotta pots. Just before they reached the door, they passed a young woman walking by in the opposite direction who dropped her shawl. Hugo, never one to forgo an opportunity like that where a pretty young woman was concerned, picked it up and handed it back to her, taking care to run an admiring eye up and down her slim, attractive figure.

As they reached the door of the restaurant, he cast a furtive glance down the street, just in time to see the girl entering some oriental eatery nearby. Titillating thoughts flashed through his mind. Pity her name wasn't Belcanto, he mused. It'd be fun to be taking her out to dinner. But enough of these distractions! He must concentrate his mind on the business in hand, the seduction of poor – or rather rich – little Lisa, his passport, he hoped, to financial security, comfort and the good life.

Wednesday 2nd June 1801

Of course, Antonin did not know then that the course of his life was about to change forever. The chain of events which would lead to this sudden alteration in his fortunes had started one early summer morning, quite innocently – or at least relatively innocently, innocence in Antonin's case being a rather relative term.

He had decided to take a stroll in Vauxhall Pleasure Gardens. He loved the beautiful tree-lined walks, fountains, statues, colonnades and miscellaneous attractions. He would have gone there more often if the entrance fee hadn't been a full two shillings. Today, though, he had just been paid by one of his patrons for a month's worth of piano lessons and thought he deserved a special treat. Sometimes, if his uncle agreed to come and pay for them both, he would attend a concert in the evening or even a firework display.

That morning caught him in a more than usually contented mood. Recently, he had at last moved into rooms of his own in Bloomsbury, and though paying the rent was always a struggle, he enjoyed the feeling of independence which having his own abode gave him. Further, a meeting with two other musicians, also recent immigrants from his homeland, had led to the formation of a piano trio. He entertained high hopes of engagements to play at grand houses for fashionable society gatherings, which would give him the chance to show off his pianistic talents. The opportunity might even arise, he thought, for the trio to play at a public concert at the Hannover Square Rooms, where some of Haydn's own symphonies were first performed.

He had another reason, too, to be optimistic about the future, something really quite extraordinary, which he was keeping to himself for the present, but which he dared to hope might be the means to secure his future and enable him to give up the tedious music lessons upon which for the moment his livelihood depended.

As he passed by Handel's statue, he whistled to himself a

melody from the famous Music for the Royal Fireworks which Handel had composed more than half a century before and was, he discovered, first rehearsed in these very pleasure gardens. Apparently, an immense crowd had attended to hear the rehearsal and traffic had blocked London Bridge for several hours.

He hadn't walked much further when the skies produced some unexpected firework music of their own. It had been fine enough when he began his stroll, but dark clouds had bubbled up from nowhere. There was a spectacular flash of lightning and a booming clap of thunder which were soon followed by a heavy shower. He took refuge in one of the colonnades nearby, and found himself standing close to two ladies who had also taken shelter there. They were in animated conversation together and Antonin edged nearer in an attempt to ensure that he was clearly in the line of sight of the prettier and younger of the two. Sure enough she cast him a glance before abruptly turning her head away. A few moments later she did the same again, much as Magdalena Malinska had done at the musical soirée to celebrate her wedding anniversary nearly five years before. Patiently he waited to see what might ensue. He had a feeling that something would, and he was rarely wrong in such matters.

And something did – the pretty young lady dropped a handkerchief. It was about the oldest ploy that a young lady might adopt in seeking to attract the attention of a gentleman but still one of the easiest and most effective. Whatever the outcome might be, there could be no conceivable embarrassment for either party. Most enterprising schemes entail an element of risk, but in this case, nothing need be ventured beyond the risk of a soiled handkerchief if the ground were wet or muddy and everything might be gained if the gentleman willingly took the bait. Antonin sensed immediately that the handkerchief had been dropped deliberately despite the casual artifice with which it had been done, and this in turn led him to suspect that it was not the first time that the young lady in question had dropped a handkerchief in the park.

He stooped and retrieved the article from where it had come to rest, near his right foot, and turned to face the ladies.

"Please pardon my intrusion, madam, but I believe this is yours," he said, addressing the pretty young lady. Antonin's English was now almost perfect. Like many musicians he was a natural linguist though he retained a strong central European accent which most English people, especially the womenfolk, seemed to find amusing and which he therefore took some trouble to exaggerate.

"Why, thank you, sir. Indeed, it is. How careless of me! It is one of a set of six given to me by my dear Aunt Lucy. Best Honiton lace too. I should be quite mortified to have lost it."

"I am most pleased to have been of service," he said with one of his exceptionally beguiling smiles.

"Do I detect that you are a foreigner, sir? Although, may I say, you speak English uncommonly well," the young lady asked, sounding quite beguiled already.

"You are entirely correct, madam. I am from Prague. If I may be permitted to introduce myself. My name is Antonin Vasylicek and I am a musician by profession," Antonin replied, bowing gracefully.

"Well, my name is Emma Cathcart and this is my sister, Mrs. Gloria Finchley."

"I am enchanted to meet you," Antonin said, addressing himself to Gloria.

"But not, methinks, nearly so enchanted as you are to have met my sister," Gloria replied somewhat sharply. "Now, come along, Emma. Your husband will be wondering what has happened to us." There was an appreciable stress laid on the word 'husband'.

"But it is still raining, and I shall wet my new bonnet," Emma protested.

"The rain is much eased, and in any event, what do you suppose is the purpose of a bonnet if not to protect your head from the elements?"

"But not necessarily so, sister, not if there is alternative shelter, surely."

"Ladies, I do believe the rain will soon cease if we are all patient a few moments longer."

"Oh, very well," Gloria said, huffily resigning herself to wait.

"Did I understand you to say that you are a musician, sir?" Emma asked, resuming the conversation.

"Yes, indeed."

"Perhaps we might arrange a musical evening for you to come and play for us at Brook Street where we are staying with my sister-in-law, Lady Melchett. She is a great devotee of the arts and would, I know, be most pleased. I am sure that it would be a most agreeable occasion."

"I should be delighted," Antonin said, quite genuinely delighted and for more than one reason.

"Don't be silly, Emma," Gloria cut in. "We are hardly acquainted with this gentleman. For all that we know he may play the hurdy-gurdy or some other raucous instrument popular with the common people. Besides we go to Bath on Friday, had you forgotten? There is no time to organise musical entertainments, foolish girl."

Emma quite lost her sparkle for a moment, but soon rallied.

"Why, sir, you should come to Bath yourself. Everyone goes to Bath for the season. There are many fine concerts and I am sure you would find a visit very rewarding. Taking the waters of the spa is also most beneficial for one's health and I strongly commend it to you. Oh, you really should come, sir. You will find us at the

Pump Room or the Assembly Rooms most days."

"Come along, Emma. The rain has quite stopped now."

"Goodbye, sir, and thank you once again. Perchance, we may see you in Bath."

"Goodbye."

Antonin watched them both walk away, before himself turning to walk in the other direction. He had no intention then of taking up Emma's suggestion of visiting Bath, but had much enjoyed their brief encounter. He always enjoyed the company of a pretty young woman, particularly if a little flirtation was on offer.

Later that day, he went to see his Uncle Jan at The Bell and Candle. He returned, in fact, most days to The Bell and Candle, not only for the sake of his uncle's company, but to practise his playing of the fortepiano. Jan possessed a more or less serviceable instrument in his private rooms at the rear of the inn, of which he was happy for Antonin to avail himself. Thinking it might amuse his uncle, he mentioned his meeting with Emma and Gloria that afternoon in Vauxhall Gardens and Emma's suggestion that he should visit Bath.

"But you should certainly go to Bath, Antonin," his uncle insisted. "It is a spa town as renowned for its beauty as for the quality of its waters. Your pretty young admirer was right. Fashionable society flock to see and be seen there. There are concerts, theatre, parties – all manner of attractions. Who knows whom you may meet and what good fortune may follow."

Tuesday 28th September 2004

Pouring himself another pre-prandial glass of vintage Pol Roger, Hugo mused upon his good fortune.

Just over two months had passed since Hugo had taken Lisa to dinner at Chez Véronique on the pretext of interviewing her for a magazine article. Frankly, the thing had more or less been in the bag after the first Bellini cocktail, but Hugo had thought it judicious not to rush things too much. The fish was securely hooked, no point in reeling it in too fast and risking it getting off before it was safely in the net. He left it a good week before asking her out to dinner again. After that, he gradually increased the pace. They began to see more and more of each other until finally, two weeks ago, he had moved into her delightful little cottage in a cobbled mews just north of Hyde Park, and arranged to let his own place in Earls Court.

Hugo had actually become quite fond of Lisa after a fashion. Though, being Hugo, this may have had much to do with the fact that she was a singularly undemanding young woman. She rarely nagged him about anything, and there were no awkward questions if he came home late or went out for the evening. This of course suited his book completely. He was able to live a life not too far removed from his old routine – he could visit his club and see his friends more or less whenever he pleased, and generally indulge himself in much the same manner as he always had.

Nobody would maintain that Lisa was a real beauty, but she was certainly not unattractive, and, although no competition for some of his racier girlfriends, matters in the bedroom department were not totally unsatisfactory. In any case, if he desired a little extra entertainment there was always Sadie, a barmaid at a favourite wine bar, who had always been a reliable stand-by. She was usually game for a bit of uncomplicated fun and if by chance she wasn't available… well, there were other old girlfriends he could call on. He only had to tell poor Lisa that he had to review some opera or concert performance somewhere, and she would be none the wiser.

More to the point and central to his scheme, Lisa had proved, just as he had hoped, to be more than generous with cash. She was always buying him new shirts, expensive shoes, designer label ties, gold cufflinks, the latest electronic gizmos and much more besides. More significantly, she paid all the bills at the cottage and did all the necessary shopping without asking Hugo for any contribution at all towards the cost. He lived essentially free at Lisa's expense, whilst continuing to enjoy rent from his own flat, rent which more or less covered his mortgage repayments. She treated him to regular dinners at expensive restaurants and paid for a luxurious long weekend at the Danieli Hotel in Venice, with first-class flights there and back. The income he enjoyed from his critical reviews and journalism was available for him to fritter away as he pleased. He was no longer dependent on it for his livelihood.

In fact, if Hugo needed anything more, anything at all, all he had to do was to ask. As a result, his financial position had already improved beyond recognition. No more unpleasant letters from the bank complaining that he had exceeded his overdraft limit, no more staggering credit card bills, no more having to make do with second best, no more cheap hotels, second-class travel or second-rate champagne.

As an added bonus, Lisa was an excellent cook. That day, they were having an evening at home and Hugo was much looking forward to his supper.

"Hugo," she said, as they sat down to eat.

"Yes, my love?"

"Dad and Gina would like to meet you."

"Oh, that would be nice. I suppose that means a trip up north?" Hugo knew that there was a family home somewhere near Wilmslow, not far from Manchester where the swish head office of the business was based.

Lisa's father, Hugo understood, had acquired there a three-acre site, upon which he had had designed and built a large Italianate villa, called Syracuse Lodge, comprising, according to Lisa, eight bedrooms and including, amongst its numerous facilities, a gymnasium, solarium, an indoor swimming pool with sauna and Jacuzzi, tennis courts and an ornamental lake.

"No, no, Dad is coming down on Friday to stay with Gina for the weekend at the company flat. We've been invited to dinner there on Friday evening."

Hugo knew that Frank's company maintained an apartment in London where Gina, the stepmother, seemed to spend most of her time, but he had never been invited there before, nor yet indeed met Gina.

"Oh… splendid!"

Lisa did not appear to be very close to her stepmother and only rarely visited her, but he knew that she thought the world of her father. This dinner could well be crucial and it was imperative that he gave a good impression. He was confident, though, that his natural charm would, as always, win the day.

All in all, the grand plan was proceeding very well, very well indeed.

Monday 15th June 1801

Antonin had decided after all to take his uncle's advice and travel to Bath. Uncle Jan might be right. There could be a world of wonderful opportunities waiting for him there, but if he was really honest with himself, it was the prospect of meeting young Emma Cathcart again that was the true motivation for his visit. His uncle's suggestion merely provided a convenient excuse to justify the expense which naturally he could ill afford. He would worry about that later, though.

He had made a few discreet enquiries before leaving London and had been able to ascertain that Lady Melchett, whom Emma had referred to as her sister-in-law resident in Brook Street, had a brother called Sir Willoughby Cathcart, a country squire living in Somerset. It appeared that she had no other brothers and thus Sir Willoughby must be Emma's husband, as indeed he was.

The Cathcarts lived at Tresham Manor, a large Tudor house in the Blackdown Hills of the Somersetshire countryside. Sir Willoughby, wary that marital duties might not always sit easily with his hunting, gambling and drinking habits, had remained a bachelor until late in life. Only the need to produce an heir had driven him finally towards the thought of matrimony. He had scoured the county for a suitable bride but in vain. Of course, there was many a lady still capable of child-bearing who, through a lack of a sufficient dowry or comely enough features, had failed yet to secure a husband and would gladly have accepted a man of his wealth and position. However, Sir Willoughby was determined to share his bed with a pretty young woman, if he had to share it with anyone. What was the point, after all, of going huntin' and choosin' an old nag for a ride? Better surely an eager young mount able to keep up with the field and rarin' to jump the hedges and ditches! The same principle surely applied to one's choice of spouse, he reasoned.

If he was going to marry, then he would make sure to have some jolly fine sport out of it. He was deuced if he wouldn't!

By a happy chance he was taking tea one day at the vicarage with the Very Reverend Josiah Finchley, the local Rector, and his wife Gloria, when Emma, Gloria's younger sister, happened by. Sir Willoughby was immediately taken with Emma's good looks and charm and without a moment's hesitation concluded that she was the one for him! Indeed, she was the most captivating young filly he'd ever cast a rheumy old eye over with her soft peachy skin and pretty face, not to mention a damn fine brace of tits and a saucy little wiggle in her stride. By God, he was damned if a man could do any better and he was quite determined to take her for his wife.

On the very next morning he proposed marriage, and, after the shortest of intervals consistent with due propriety, she accepted him.

The delightful Miss Emma was just nineteen years old whilst Sir Willoughby, his face as old and gnarled as the ancient oak tree which stood in the courtyard of Tresham Manor, was a man of nearly seventy summers. It was a picture with which Antonin was all too familiar and had exploited with great success on many a previous occasion: to wit a bored young wife yearning for a little excitement with a handsome young buck. Well, never fear, he would provide the required excitement.

Arriving in Bath late on a Monday, somewhat weary and dishevelled after the long journey, he was fortunate enough to find a cheap room in a lodging house in the lower part of the town. He would, he decided, wait until the following morning before setting out to pursue his quarry.

Friday 1st October 2004

The Belcanto Continental flat where Gina, the stepmother, lived, turned out to be within easy walking reach of Lisa's cottage. It was in a smart redbrick apartment block in Bayswater built during the thirties called Beacon Court. Hugo wondered why Frank had bought Lisa a house of her own when she came to London. Surely she could have shared this place with her stepmother, he thought. Presumably money was no object. But there was a good reason.

The flat was one of the two penthouse apartments in the block and a large old-fashioned-style lift chugged its way sedately to the top of the building. The lift door slid open to reveal a pleasant wide lobby area on the opposite side of which were two matching doors to the respective penthouses, and the one on the right was almost immediately opened by a tall, well-built man with dark oily hair swept back and greying at the temples, very dark eyes, and a large, square, slightly protruding chin.

"Hi, Dad," Lisa said, "hope we're not too early."

"No, it's fine," he said, stooping to kiss his daughter. "And you must be Hugo," he continued, half turning to face him. He spoke in a deep, gravelly voice with an accent which was not quite Italian not quite Mancunian but a curious mixture of both.

"Yes, sir."

"Come on in then."

He led them into a small hallway. Lisa was sent off to join her stepmother in the kitchen, while Frank and Hugo proceeded through an open doorway into a large drawing room.

Hugo was quite astonished by the opulent fashion in which the room was furnished. He had expected something bland and corporate, but here was a riot of Art Deco splendour upon which absolutely no expense had been spared: Lalique glassware and table lamps vied for attention with bronze and ivory figurines of dancing girls on a long low cabinet shaped a bit like an ocean liner. On one side of the French window leading to the sun terrace stood a superb bulbous black lacquered chiffonier and on the other side an elaborate bronze and iron screen. A magnificent Cartier clock in an ancient Egyptian style dominated the mantelpiece matching the design of the sofas and chairs. Not only did it all tone perfectly with the age and character of the building, but the place, Hugo mused, could easily have served as a stage set for a particularly lavish production of a Noël Coward play.

As Hugo stood reeling in amazement as he took in his surroundings, Frank thrust a glass of Prosecco into his hand and waved him to a seat. Frank himself, however, remained standing, which put Hugo at an instant disadvantage. Frank seemed an even larger and more forbidding figure than he had when he had greeted them at the door. There was about him an aura of ruthless power. He looked down at Hugo, casting upon him one of those merciless, penetrating stares which men of his stamp always seemed to possess as a necessary implement of their authority. Indeed, it seemed to Hugo that Frank's stare, as far as merciless and penetrating stares go, was at the very top end of the range. Hugo's old friend Archie had warned him that Frank was 'no ordinary bastard', and though Hugo was not normally a man of nervous disposition, he could not help but feel somewhat ill at ease now.

"Remind me what you do for a living, Hugo," Frank asked, with an emphasis on the word 'Hugo' in a tone of voice which suggested that he didn't think much of it as a name.

"I'm a freelance music critic and journalist, sir."

"You write for the newspapers?"

"Well newspapers and magazines, yes… mainly reviews and sometimes articles on cultural or other topics of contemporary interest, that sort of thing."

"I see… and what was the last of these, er, reviews about, then?"

"Oh, a performance of 'Così Fan Tutte' at the Coliseum, about a week ago."

"That a show?"

"Well, it's an opera by Mozart."

"Oh, Mozart… one of those dead composers, isn't he?"

"Yes, sir, um, quite right."

"The only composer I know about is Verdi. He's dead, too, of course, but he was an Italian, you know. My father used to sing songs from Verdi operas all the time when I was a kid. 'La donna e mobile' and all those other tunes. You know 'em, I suppose?"

"Yes, of course, very much so. Verdi has always been a great favourite of mine."

"Good, good. Now, where were we? Oh yeah, your job. So, these papers and magazines actually pay for you to write stuff about operas composed by these dead people, then?"

"Well, yes… actually they do."

"Beats me what people will pay good money for these days! Now, you're walking out with my daughter, is that right?"

"Yes, sir."

"Lisa's very precious to me, Hugo. You just make sure you're good to her, treat her right… and no fooling around, know what I mean?"

"Lisa has become very precious to me too, sir, even in the short time I've known her," Hugo replied, deciding to treat the 'fooling around' bit as a rhetorical question to which no particular answer was required.

"Yeah… Well, you just remember what I said."

As Frank uttered these last words, he lowered his voice to an even deeper register and spoke very slowly and deliberately. It was impossible to ignore the none too subtle hint of menace in his tone.

"You need have no fears, sir, I can assure you."

An ability to appear trustworthy and sincere is of course a vital weapon in the armoury of any successful rogue, and Hugo had honed his skills in this area to perfection, and he certainly needed them now. Frank fixed him with one of those dreadful stares for a full five seconds and then, for the first time during their conversation, he smiled. It was not exactly a radiant smile. There was no real warmth about it, but at least it was a smile.

"Okay, then," he said.

At this moment, Lisa entered the room followed by her stepmother.

One look at her was enough for Hugo. Gina Belcanto was, without the faintest flicker of a doubt, the most ravishing woman he had ever set eyes on, even allowing for the fact that every attractive woman he met always seemed to him at the time to be 'the most ravishing woman he had ever set eyes on'. He was realistic enough, of course, to know that his libidinous nature had this effect on him, just as a glass or two of champagne tended to induce in him the feeling that in the great steeplechase of life his metaphorical horse had just won the Grand National. But even allowing for the drug-like effects of his overactive libido, Hugo knew then that he desired Gina more than any other woman he had ever seen before, even though they had only just met each other and not a word had passed between them.

"What a pleasure to meet you, Hugo, at last," Gina said in a distinctly upper-class accent. Hugo was surprised. He had assumed, quite wrongly, that she would have come from the same sort of background as her husband. "Lisa has been keeping you all to herself for far too long!"

As Gina spoke, she advanced towards Hugo, leant forward and kissed him delicately on both cheeks, squeezing his hand in hers as she did so. Drawing back from each other, they exchanged the briefest of glances, but it was enough – enough for Gina to know exactly what Hugo was thinking and enough, too, for Hugo to know that Gina's thoughts were running along precisely similar lines. It was for both of them simply a case of lust at first sight.

"Come along now, dinner is ready."

They moved through double doors from the drawing room into a smaller dining area furnished in much the same style.

Gina proved to be an even better cook than Lisa, and there were well-chosen wines to match each course. The occasion itself, though, was not a great success. There was an air of awkwardness about it which impeded the flow of conversation. Hugo, socially adept as he undoubtedly was, had rescued many a dinner party from disaster in his time, but this one was quite beyond him.

Gina made a brief attempt to discuss a play she had been to see recently in the West End, but it was quite obvious that Frank had no interest whatever in the theatre and her valiant effort to get things going rapidly petered out. Apart from some disparaging remarks about current food and hygiene regulations, the iniquities of the tax system, and the late arrival of his train from Manchester, Frank remained, for the most part, sullen and uncommunicative. Lisa, however, seemingly quite oblivious to the pervasive sense of unease, chattered away inconsequentially. At least, Hugo thought, her prattle helped to cover up what otherwise might have been a series of long, embarrassing silences.

If only Frank hadn't been there, Hugo felt sure that the evening would have been a very different affair, and an exchange of glances with Gina indicated to him that she was of like mind. As it was, he was thoroughly relieved when it was finally over and time to go home.

"Goodnight, Hugo darling. I think Daddy really liked you."

"And I liked him very much, too – charming man. Goodnight, my sweet."

Lisa turned over and fell asleep almost immediately, but Hugo remained stubbornly awake, pondering the events of the evening. Frank was plainly a difficult character, worse even than he had imagined or his friend Archie had warned. He would have to watch his step. Mainly, though, his thoughts revolved around the gorgeous Gina, thoughts which, being Hugo, rapidly turned towards sexual fantasy. But might fantasy, he dared to wonder, conceivably become reality? Somehow instinctively he felt that it would not be long before he heard from Gina again. What an extraordinary, but rather splendid thought!

Gina also lay awake that night beside the somnolent, snoring bulk of her husband Frank. Could this handsome, charming man Hugo, with whom she had exchanged such meaningful glances, possibly be the missing piece in life's jigsaw? She speculated. It was an intriguing idea!

Tuesday 16th June 1801

Antonin set out early to explore Bath. A short walk brought him to the Pump Room, but the Cathcarts were not to be seen there. Not unduly concerned, Antonin decided to spend some time investigating the delights of the city before further pursuing his quest.

The Assembly Rooms, at which Antonin arrived later that day, comprised four large, elegant rooms: the Octagon, the Card Room, the Ballroom and the Tea Room. He concluded that the Cathcarts were as likely as not to be found in the Tea Room and such indeed proved to be the case. Looking about the room, he noticed them almost at once sitting alone at a table in a corner. Emma happened to glance in his direction at that very moment and motioned enthusiastically for him to join them.

"My dearest, this is the kind gentleman who recently performed such a great service for me in the park in London. Allow me, sir, to introduce my husband."

Sir Willoughby grunted by way of acknowledgement.

"Antonin Vasylicek, sir, at your service. I am indeed privileged to make your acquaintance."

"Please do be seated, sir," Emma said, indicating an empty chair, an invitation of which Antonin was quick to take advantage. He was relieved that there was no sign of Emma's sister Gloria.

"And what, pray, was the nature of this singular service that was so important to you, my dear?" Sir Willoughby asked.

"Why, my dear, did I not tell you about it? This gentleman retrieved a precious lace handkerchief which my clumsy fingers carelessly let slip to the ground."

"Scarce a matter of life and death, what?"

"But important to me, my dearest. It is a favourite handkerchief of Honiton lace and I should be fair desolate to have lost it."

"Ah, well, then, we must thank this gentleman for his trouble in rescuing you from such a dreadful misfortune!"

"My dear," Emma continued, endeavouring to change the subject, "Mr Vassily… forgive me, sir, but I cannot order my poor tongue properly to pronounce your name… is a musician from… from… Oh dear, I forget quite where."

"The city of Prague."

"Why yes, of course, Prague."

Sir Willoughby was at a loss to understand quite why he should share his table with some foreign handkerchief retriever, however musical he might be. In any case the calling of a musician, in his view, was not very far removed from that of any ordinary tradesman. Butchers, bakers and candlestick makers are purveyors of beef, bread and candlesticks while musicians purvey notes and melodies; what was the difference? However, for Emma's sake, he resolved to be patient and tolerate the fellow's intrusion.

"I suppose you come to Bath, sir, to blow your trumpet?" he said, unable to avoid entirely a hint of the sarcastic condescension with which he was wont to address those of inferior social status.

"No, Sir. I come purely for the purposes of pleasure, indeed on your own dear wife's recommendation."

Sir Willoughby was about to reply something along the lines that the music trade must be uncommonly profitable these days, when he was interrupted by a man touting the claims of a new cure for gout. The fellow was evidently a fraudulent quack, but Sir Willoughby listened with great attention. A frequent sufferer from this most painful of afflictions, he would listen to anybody promising a cure.

Whilst her husband was distracted, Emma leant over the table and, laying a hand delicately on Antonin's arm and bringing her pretty face as close to his as possible, whispered in his ear a day, a time and an address in Royal Crescent.

The day Emma had whispered was the next but one, and

Antonin had no alternative but to amuse himself as best he could until then, but at last the time arrived and at the appointed hour he duly presented himself at the house in Royal Crescent, the address of which Emma had whispered to him. The door was opened by Emma herself. Sir Willoughby had left in the morning for Bristol to visit his wine merchant and was not expected back until much later that evening; the servants had been given the day off. The sister Gloria had departed some days earlier with her dutiful husband ever anxious to resume his pastoral duties in the wilds of Somerset.

A few minutes were spent upon polite conversation of the usual inconsequential kind before Emma suggested that a splendid view of the city and surrounding countryside might be enjoyed from the second floor – would he like to see? Well, of course he would.

There was indeed a splendid view in the main bedroom on the second floor to which she led him, but it was not the view of Bath and its environs upon which he was invited to feast his eyes, but a view of a rather more intimate nature which did not involve looking out of the window at all. A moment or two later, he gathered her up in his arms and carried her giggling and squealing to the handsome four-poster bed.

So engrossed in their lovemaking were they that neither heard the heavy footfalls on the stairs; only when the door of the bedroom swung open did Antonin become aware of imminent danger. For there in the doorway stood Emma's doting husband, having returned much earlier from Bristol than expected, goggling in disbelief at the scene which met his eyes.

Antonin promptly leapt from the bed, gathered up his clothes from the floor where they lay and just managed to squeeze past the unfortunate baronet as he stood gaping and stammering in the doorway.

Rushing across the landing and pulling on his breeches and shirt as he went, he could barely recall descending the stairs or crossing the hallway; somehow, he found himself by the front door, half decently dressed, except for his coat which he was still carrying and his shoes which he realised he had left behind in the bedroom. Just then, Sir Willoughby, wits now fully restored, appeared at the top of the stairs roaring and cursing.

Wasting no further time Antonin quickly left the house, slamming shut the front door after him. Sir Willoughby was soon, however, in hot, full-throated pursuit. He was not a master of foxhounds for nothing, and his rasping rustic curses reverberated from one end of Royal Crescent to the other. He also exhibited a quite extraordinary turn of speed for a man of his age and portly girth. Poor Antonin found himself chased relentlessly the whole way to the Circus and halfway round it. He only managed finally to evade his pursuer by mingling with a large crowd gathering for a concert outside the Assembly Rooms.

The very next morning, he set off to return by mail coach to London, having purloined a fresh pair of boots from an open doorway in Queen Square the previous evening. It had been a terrifying experience and he dreaded to think what might have happened if Sir Willoughby had caught up with him. However, safely back in London, he was inclined at first to make light of the whole affair.

In view of his absence, it had been necessary to rearrange a few appointments for music lessons, and the first of these appointments fell a week later, the day after that upon which he would have returned from Bath if circumstances had not cut short his stay. His pupil on this occasion was the wife of a wealthy man of business, residing in Bedford Square. Antonin arrived at the house in good time. A manservant answered and informed him that his master had given the strictest instruction that on no account was he to be admitted. It was the same everywhere.

News of the scandal involving Emma Cathcart had travelled quickly and Antonin found door after door barred to him. Respectable folk, once aware of what had taken place in Bath, would hardly countenance such a rogue to cross their threshold, let alone anywhere near their wives and daughters as they practised their scales and arpeggios. Many, of course, were secretly rather jealous and would not have spurned an opportunity of a tryst with Emma themselves, if the matter could have been managed discreetly; but, dammit all, this fellow was a mere music teacher, scarcely better than a servant, and a foreign one to boot!

The incident in Bath heralded the end of Antonin's brief and hardly glorious career in England. To make matters worse, he was in substantial debt, as always, and present circumstances deprived him of the means to earn a living, or to make any repayment to his creditors. Less than a month after his return to the city, he heard that the bailiffs were out looking for him. Unable to settle his debts, no doubt they would haul him off to the debtors' prison – a fate altogether too awful to contemplate. According to the friend who had brought him this disturbing news, the bailiffs had already visited his lodgings. He had fortunately been elsewhere when they came, but it would surely only be a matter of time before they caught up with him. He must leave at once.

Feverishly, he gathered up his few possessions and made haste to depart. He would spend the night at his uncle's inn, and decide where best to go thereafter.

"So," Uncle Jan said, after Antonin had advised him of his present predicament and of its likely outcome if the bailiffs caught up with him, "you'll be on your travels again, I suppose. You'll need some money. I'll give you some tomorrow."

"Many thanks, uncle. You have always been very kind to me."

"I've got some news for you too, Antonin… I am leaving

London for the countryside."

"This is very sudden, uncle," Antonin replied, genuinely surprised. "You gave me no indication of this the last time I met with you."

"Sudden indeed it was, and, until I had finally decided, I felt it best to keep the matter a secret. Just after you left for Bath, I went to a concert of Haydn's music at the King's Theatre in the Haymarket, and suffered a near accident. It was not the first time I had nearly suffered an accident after the performance of a work by Haydn. I recall some years ago, I attended the premiere of one of his symphonies, at which the old master himself was present, and a chandelier fell from the ceiling and might have killed me had I not by good fortune just vacated my seat. This time it was a woman…"

"A woman falling from the ceiling!?"

"Well, not exactly from the ceiling. She tripped on the stairs and nearly bowled me over. I managed to catch her arm as she fell and probably saved her from injury. Both she and her husband, Squire Pemberton, who was descending just behind her when she fell, were most grateful for my timely intervention. The Squire invited me to call the next day at his brother's house in Chelsea where they were staying. The Squire is a very direct sort of gentleman, not one, as I believe the English hunting fraternity are wont to say, to 'beat around the bush'. On learning that I was an innkeeper, he made me an offer."

"An offer?"

"You see the innkeeper of the Pemberton Arms recently broke his back when he fell off a horse…"

"This seems to be a tale woefully full of accidents."

"Yes, I suppose it is, but then life itself is simply a series of accidents, is it not? What if you hadn't by chance met your young friend Emma in Vauxhall Gardens, for example? Some accidents bring forth bad luck, some good. In your case, catastrophe! In my case, the unfortunate accident suffered by the innkeeper of the Pemberton Arms resulted in the Squire's kind offer."

"But, uncle, what is the nature of this offer?"

"That I become the new innkeeper of the Pemberton Arms. The freehold of the inn is owned by the Pemberton estate. Indeed, the estate extends to most of the local village and its outlying farms. The inn stands on the drovers' road right next to the drive which leads to Pemberton Hall itself, where the Squire and his family live. The Squire offered me a lease of the inn at an exceedingly modest rent, and the lease also includes the lodge house, known as West Lodge, which lies on the other side of the main gates to the drive. You may recall that I was away all last week – Well, I made a journey to the country to visit this place. It is not too far from London but life is very different there. The inn has been a well-known coaching inn for centuries and enjoys a very profitable trade. I decided there and then to accept the Squire's offer. West Lodge, which is indeed a most delightful and commodious property, will be our home…"

"Our home?"

"Why yes, of course, Mary and I."

"Mary?"

"Mary, you know, who serves here at the inn."

"Mary is coming with you, then?"

"Oh, did I omit to inform you?" Antonin's uncle replied, a little bashfully. "Mary and I are to be married."

"Married, eh!" Antonin smiled as he tried to visualise Mary, the amply-bosomed barmaid, in her bridal gown. "But isn't she a little young for you, Uncle Jan?"

"An old man must have his consolations, Antonin."

" Indeed!"

"Mary has a very…" Uncle Jan continued, doing his best to

ignore Antonin's interruption.

"…splendid bosom?!"

"Warm heart! You lewd scoundrel!"

"I'm sure, uncle," Antonin said, adopting a more serious tone, "that Mary will bring you great happiness, and that the Pemberton Arms will prosper under your excellent stewardship. I congratulate you on your good fortune."

"Thank you, my dear fellow. Although chance has not been so kind to you, your luck will change, you may depend on it."

"I hope so, uncle!"

That night at The Bell and Candle, fitfully turning this way and that, unable to sleep, Antonin wondered what the future might hold for him. Would he settle one day at last, like his Uncle Jan, for an ordered life of work, respectability and conjugal commitment, or was he destined to spend the rest of his days flitting from place to place, seducing impressionable young ladies whilst ordering elaborately embroidered waistcoats for which he could ill afford to pay?

Monday 4th October 2004

"How would you like to come round for a coffee?"

"I'd love to, Gina," Hugo replied. "I shall be with you in two ticks."

The telephone had rung shortly after 9.30am. Before he had even picked up the receiver, he just knew it would be Gina.

Lisa had left for work, the art gallery where Gina worked was closed on Mondays, and Frank would, doubtlessly, be safely on the train to Manchester. It could not be better.

Less than twenty minutes later, Hugo was pressing the button on the entry phone at Beacon Court for Gina's apartment. Gina let him in and he took the lift to the top floor. It seemed to take an agonisingly long time to get up there, longer even than it had on his first visit, and, when it finally arrived, there was a frustratingly long pause before the lift door eventually slid back open.

It was all worth it, however. Gina was there in the lobby waiting for him. She looked even more spectacularly gorgeous than he remembered. He was about to say something to this effect, but she put a finger to his lips to silence him, and turned on her heel. Hugo followed obediently behind her into the apartment and thence through the hallway to the master bedroom.

There was no sign of a coffee pot.

Later, over a light lunch swiftly prepared by Gina and a bottle of champagne, they talked. It turned out to be a most illuminating conversation in which they both came to realise just how much they had in common. Both were roughly the same age, in their mid-thirties. Gina's husband Frank was nearly sixty.

Both came from well-educated, upper middle-class backgrounds, but in neither case was there much money. Gina's parents, both retired college lecturers, lived in genteel poverty in the country near Hereford, whilst Hugo's widowed mother lived in Oxfordshire in a rambling pair of converted weavers' cottages knocked into one, subsisting on a widow's pension augmented only by a modest income from a family trust, the capital of which had been sadly depleted over the years by school fees and other costs.

Both desired comfort and financial security with ready access to the good things of life, but each had come to the conclusion that there must be an easier route to obtain this desirable state of affairs than the tedious business of hard work. The obvious solution was an age-old one – marry money!

Hugo had good looks, wit and abundant charm, while Gina had a fabulous figure, a sexy voice and a most alluring smile. With great determination, each had set about deploying these valuable assets to attract a suitably wealthy spouse.

Gina used to work at the same PR consultancy firm as Lisa. She had flirted outrageously with Frank as he waited one day in reception for a meeting. She knew from her boss that Belcanto Continental was one of the firm's most valuable accounts. Frank, she could see, was totally besotted with her, and he wasted no time in inviting her out to dinner. Soon they began regularly going out together. Not only did Gina arouse Frank's earthier instincts as never before, but she seemed to him the ideal 'trophy wife' for which he had long been searching. A wife of Gina's obvious class and beauty would surely confirm that he had truly arrived. She would, he thought, ideally complement the big luxury mansion, the swanky offices, the sharp suits, the stable of expensive motorcars and all the rest. Naturally, he was anxious to close the deal as soon as possible, and proposed marriage to her after only a month from their first date.

Gina, however, fully aware of Frank's eagerness, chose to play it cool. Now was the opportunity, she recognised, to state her terms, and she drove a very hard bargain indeed...

First and foremost, of course, she expected a generous regular allowance. £15 thousand a month was the barest minimum and that was on the basis that Frank or his company in addition would pay all her living costs and domestic bills. Surely nothing less would be appropriate to her status as the wife of the chairman, chief executive and principal shareholder of a hugely successful business, would it now?

A measure of freedom and independence was, she insisted, of great importance to her. Under no circumstances was she prepared to live full time with Frank at this place of his near Manchester. London must remain her home base, where all her friends lived. She would leave her poky little flat in Putney, and take up residence at the company's spacious apartment overlooking Hyde Park. The apartment would need total refurbishment, naturally to be undertaken entirely at the company's expense, but in a manner which suited her taste. The company Mercedes kept in the basement car park would be at her disposal at all times except when needed by Frank or one of his co-executives visiting London (actually rarely required).

Naturally, Frank – as her husband, after all – could come and stay whenever he pleased (in practice, this boiled down, as Gina had guessed that it would, to no more than one weekend in three).

Provided Frank was prepared to pick up the tab for completely updating her wardrobe, Gina would be quite happy to play the elegant hostess at business dinners and drinks parties held at the apartment and would duly charm the socks off Frank's guests (in fact, these events happened no more than four or five times a year).

Frank's proposal that Gina should share the apartment with Lisa when she came down to London to work was roundly rejected – Gina absolutely must have her own personal space... Hence the purchase of Lisa's mews cottage which Hugo now, to all intents and purposes, counted as home.

Gina would leave her job at the PR firm. A secretarial role would hardly be consistent with her new position in life, but she was too young and intelligent simply to do nothing at all. She needed some part-time interest which would keep her in touch with the world and prevent her from becoming bored. A friend had suggested going into partnership together in an art gallery business in South Kensington, specialising in Japanese water-colours. This seemed a most suitable venture. Frank – gulp! – would of course be required to advance the necessary capital.

Finally, there must be a pre-nuptial agreement which would guarantee Gina's financial position in the event of a marriage breakdown. Biting his lip, Frank lamely accepted Gina's proposals, with very few concessions on her part, and Gina agreed to become his wife.

The wedding and reception were held some months later in a fairytale castle, as the glossy brochure inevitably described it, on the heather-clad banks of a Scottish loch, from which, as the festivities drew to a close, a specially chartered seaplane whisked the happy couple away to the warmer waters of Lake Garda in Italy, where they were to spend their honeymoon.

If Gina had achieved her objective, Hugo was poised to do likewise. Like a killer whale eyeing up a hapless seal pup, he was ready to move in for the kill. The time was now ripe, he judged, to propose to Lisa. Gina thought so too, and urged him to get on with it with all speed. All it needed was just the right moment to strike.

Neither of them, it has to be said, felt a smidgen of shame at the prospect of living for years at someone else's expense, nor about how this was being achieved; nor did either exhibit a glimmer of guilt about the affair upon which they had now embarked or the dreadful double betrayal they were committing.

Gina smiled one of her most alluring smiles, to which Hugo responded with one of his trademark charming grins. There was ample time, they agreed, for another visit to the bedroom before it would be time for Hugo to return to the cottage to greet his soon-to-be fiancée with a loving kiss to welcome her home from work.

Monday 20th July 1801

Some days after his hurried escape from London, Antonin found himself in the Flemish town of Bruges, and it was there at a hostelry, close to the old Augustinians' bridge, that he realised that he had left behind at his rooms in Bloomsbury something very precious to him, very precious indeed… Too bad! There could be no turning back – not now, not ever.

Wednesday 27th October 2004

"Hugo, dear boy, many congratulations on your engagement!" said Roger.

"Yes, indeed," Jeremy joined in. "My congratulations, too, and all the best!"

"Well, thanks, chaps!" Hugo replied. "Thank you very much… and it's really nice to see you both again, and very kind of you to suggest lunch."

Some two weeks before, Hugo had become formally engaged to Lisa with her father's blessing. The wedding was scheduled to take place in June the following year. Hugo had hoped for a repeat of the Scottish castle experience, but Frank had other ideas. The marriage service itself was to be celebrated in a rather ugly Catholic church on the outskirts of Manchester, while the reception would be held a few miles away in a marquee erected in the garden of Frank's home, Syracuse Lodge. The guest list would of course include many of his important customers and business associates and Frank's palatial villa with its extensive park-like grounds was to be a showcase to demonstrate his wealth and importance, much in the same way that powerful merchant princes in Renaissance Italy built gorgeous palaces, fabulous churches and other architectural splendours to demonstrate theirs. The current plans for the event included a six-course candlelit dinner, a band with some famous Italian singer, and of course an enormous firework display. Hugo thought the whole thing would be quite appalling, but he would just have to grit his teeth and look happy. It was all in a very good cause, after all.

Hugo had met up with his two old chums Roger and Jeremy at a favourite city watering hole. It was the polar opposite of one of those modern minimalist places. The decor and furnishings were plush and comfortable with warm, soothing colours and soft lighting, though not so soft that you couldn't see what you were eating. The tables were covered with crisp white linen tablecloths; the food was consistently good if not over-imaginative and the extensive wine list was well-known and much praised. Although not nearly as chic or fashionable as Chez Véronique, Hugo's favourite eating place, both he and his chums looked upon it as a 'proper' restaurant where chaps like them would feel at home.

It was a long, liquid and hugely enjoyable lunch, but all good things must come to an end, and as the waiter began clearing things away, Hugo struggled to his feet, brushing from his jacket collar a few crumbs of tarte au citron and taking a final sip of an elegantly luscious Château Rieussec.

"I won't stay for coffee, if you don't mind."

"A busy afternoon, then?"

"Let's say it promises to be an energetic one!"

"Ah… well, it's been very nice to see you, Hugo, after all this time."

As Hugo disappeared from view, one old chum turned, with a quizzical look, to address the other old chum.

"What do you suppose he meant by 'energetic', Roger? Tennis? Digging the garden or what?"

"Oh, I think I've a fair idea," Roger answered with a knowing smile.

"You know," Jeremy said, changing the subject, "I don't think we actually need to have paid for Hugo's lunch today."

"Oh?"

"Well, I carried out a bit of research, and I can tell you Hugo won't be short of a bob or two. His prospective father-in-law runs a very successful food import and distribution business. He must be a very rich man. Lisa, Hugo's fiancée, is his only child."

"Ah, I see!"

"Yes!"

Hugo stepped out onto the pavement adjacent to the restaurant to wait for his taxi. The street was one of the City's ancient charter streets, though one would hardly have guessed it now, though there was still a view of the mighty St Paul's in the distance. The street's former buildings had long disappeared, many of the earlier ones burnt down in the Great Fire, while the majority of the others were destroyed in the Blitz or demolished after the war by developers. The restaurant itself was situated in part of the ground floor of a fairly anonymous building erected in the early seventies, but a small eighteenth-century print in the gentlemen's lavatory depicted an old inn in a cobbled courtyard. A little metal plaque screwed to the wall beneath the frame was inscribed: "The Tavern, known as 'The Bell and Candle', which once occupied this site, was destroyed by enemy action in September 1940."

As Hugo waited, an elderly city gent walked slowly up the street towards him. An impish mood came over him, as it often did when he had had a little bit too much to drink. Time to have a bit of fun, he thought.

"Good afternoon, sir," he said as the gentleman drew level with him. "May I trouble you for a moment of your time?"

"I suppose so. What is it you want?"

"Well, I'm a researcher investigating sartorial trends in the contemporary working environment, and I'd like to ascertain your views."

"You're not from the BBC, are you?" the man asked suspiciously.

"No, no, of course not. I represent a voluntary organization called "Get Knotted."

"Get Knotted?!"

A lady walking the other way down the street gave them an odd look as she went by.

"Yes, you know… like knotting your tie. That's where the name of our organization originates, you see. At Get Knotted, we oppose the modern tendency for people in offices not to wear ties to work. Not only does it look terribly scruffy, but where, we ask, will it all end? Soon, people won't wear suits or even jackets. In fact, it's already happening. T-shirts and jeans or tracksuits will become the order of the day… and then why should the female staff continue to make an effort to dress properly? On hot days in summer, they'll just turn up in a thong…"

"Yes, yes…"

"You mean you'd like to see a lot of young typists in your office cavorting about in thongs, would you, you lecherous old beast?!"

"No, no, I mean I agree with you about this tie-less business."

"Good, good. Then you won't mind giving us a donation towards campaign funds… say, five hundred pounds?"

"Oh, really!"

It was perhaps fortuitous that Hugo's taxi arrived at this moment. The old man turned and walked off hurriedly up the street, muttering to himself.

"Get knotted, you bastard!" Hugo called out after him, before clambering into the back of the taxi, feeling inordinately pleased with himself.

The taxi took Hugo towards Bayswater, but not as far as Wellington Mews West where he lived with Lisa; instead, it deposited him outside Gina's apartment block. Apart from Monday when it was closed Gina worked during the week at her art gallery and greatly enjoyed it but she liked to take, not infrequently in fact, an occasional afternoon off… especially if Hugo was available…and today was such a day.

Strutting breezily the few yards to the entry phone panel, he pressed the button for the company flat.

"It's Hugo," he said, when Gina answered.

"Come on up."

On stepping out of the lift, Hugo crossed the now familiar

landing towards the flat. Finding the front door already open, he made his way to the drawing room, where Gina was waiting for him.

"Hi there, lover boy! What kept you?"

"A rather late lunch… went on a bit, I'm afraid."

"But you had one of those yesterday. Who were you with this time?"

"Oh, you know… chums."

"It was 'chums' yesterday."

"Different chums today."

"The world seems to be full of chums… I sincerely hope none of these chums are women."

"Certainly not."

"Chums can't be girlfriends, then?"

"Yes, of course they can, but not all girlfriends are chums. It depends."

"I see, and so when was the last time you had lunch with a female chum, other than our own dear Lisa?"

"Last week, if you must know."

"Last week! And who was this female, might I ask?"

"My mother. She came up to town for the day."

"Oh, I see. Well… okay. I think that's enough about your chums. Chums are boring. Let's get down to business."

And without further chit-chat, Gina led the way to the bedroom. A bottle of champagne stood in an ice bucket with two long-stemmed flutes, ready as always, to celebrate their happy exertions.

Friday 3rd December 2004

"Down, Oscar, down!"

Oscar took absolutely no notice and continued to jump up against Sandra, wagging his tail for all he was worth and barking loudly. She and Adam had just entered the great hall of Tresham Manor where they had arrived for the weekend to visit Adam's parents, Sir Arthur and Lady Edith Cathcart.

Tresham Manor, the ancestral home of the Cathcart family, nestled in a secluded valley in the Blackdown Hills of Somerset. It was built during the last years of the reign of Henry the Seventh and had not, apart from the baroque gatehouse built just after the Restoration and the mid-eighteenth-century stable block, suffered any later additions or extensions. It was accordingly regarded by architectural historians as a classic example of an English manor house of the Tudor period.

The estate enjoyed an income comprising rents from the outlying farms and cottages but it was never enough to keep up with the constant need for maintenance. The roof leaked, many of the window frames required replacement, there were cracks in the walls, rising damp, wet rot, dry rot and every other sort of rot, but the place oozed character and charm. Defying the ravages of time, weather and want of repair, the manor doggedly remained standing and more or less habitable just as its occupants had somehow managed to weather the storms of social change, buffeted but unbowed.

Sir Arthur Cathcart, Adam's father, eventually managing to restrain Oscar's enthusiasm, greeted the new arrivals.

"Adam, Sandra… good to see you both. Come and have some tea. Elsie's made a cake especially in your honour. Edith had to go down to the village hall for a meeting – something to do with the pony club apparently – but she should be back shortly."

A more genial soul than Sir Arthur would be hard to find,

though he was not without his little foibles. Shambling happily about the place in his old fishing hat, threadbare yellow cardigan and an ancient pair of cavalry twill trousers streaked with food stains, he looked, if anything, even more down at heel than his son. Edith, Lady Cathcart, to whom he had been married for close on forty years, was the daughter of a publisher. Indeed, it was her father who had founded the small publishing firm which was now run by her brother Rupert and by whom Adam was currently employed. Other than Sir Arthur and Lady Cathcart and Oscar the unruly spaniel, the rest of the ménage at the manor comprised Adam's older sister Anthea, Elsie the housekeeper and baker of cakes, Solomon the gardener and a miscellany of cats.

After his own fashion, and when he was not writing articles about salmon fishing for submission to various angling periodicals, Sir Arthur managed the estate while Edith busied herself with village affairs and kept bees. Anthea ran an 'alternative' meditation centre in part of the stable block which attracted many other-worldly but colourful folk from all over the country. Elsie, whose housekeeping duties extended to pretty much anything not done by anyone else and who had lived at Tresham almost all her adult life, was regarded as one of the family, a sort of honorary and much-loved aunt. Last but not least, Solomon looked after the manor gardens with great diligence and devotion. After several convictions for petty crime, no job and a cramped existence in a tower block in Peckham, Solomon had contemplated returning to Jamaica where there were even fewer jobs but at least the sun shone. In the event, he had got only as far as the West Country. Sir Arthur had caught him trying to break into the house through the rear pantry window, but instead of summoning the constabulary, he had offered him a job. Solomon had never looked back.

Unlike her own father, Sir Arthur certainly understood

Sandra's ambitions. Indeed, he had quite convinced himself that she was already well on her way to becoming a great opera diva.

"How goes things at the opera, my budding little Violetta?" he asked her at dinner that evening, recalling Verdi's famous courtesan. He often liked to call her that.

"Well, I haven't quite reached Covent Garden yet, Sir Arthur, if that's what, like, you mean, but I am singing in a concert in a month or so at a church hall in Hammersmith with my amateur operatic society. We're doing some arias from Handel and Mozart. A local youth orchestra is going to play for us. Perhaps someone very important will hear me sing and I shall be given a leading part at, like, La Scala or somewhere."

"Good show, good show! I'm absolutely certain you will be swamped with offers from opera houses all over Europe—"

At this point Lady Cathcart butted in.

"I'm sorry we couldn't put you in your usual room this time, my dears, but more damp got in after the recent rains, God knows from where. We've got the builders in again to deal with it. The expense of running this place is crippling. I really do think we shall have to sell up before long…"

"Sell up!? Nonsense!" Sir Arthur roared. "This house has been the Cathcart family home for over five hundred years and so it will remain, whatever the cost!"

"Couldn't we sell it to the National Trust, Pa?" Adam asked. "I mean they'd take over all the maintenance and probably let us remain as life tenants or something in part of it, wouldn't they? Isn't that what other people have done?"

"Sounds a good idea to me," Sandra chipped in.

"Certainly not!" Sir Arthur replied, quite red in the face. "I yield to no one in my admiration for the National Trust and everything they have done to preserve our national treasures, but they're not having Tresham. Can you imagine it? They'd tidy the place up and there'd be those dried flower arrangements in every room… Then of course we'd have all sorts of wretched people trudging through here on wet Sunday afternoons with their bored children. No thank you!"

"Well, if you don't want the general public here, which I must say is a little snobbish of you—"

"Snobbish?! I say, that's a bit rich coming from you, Edith, dear. Last year, you didn't even want to have the village fête on the main lawn in case someone trampled on your precious rose-beds."

"That was entirely different. In any case, it was the Elizabethan knot garden that was my main concern, especially after all the hard work poor old Solomon has put into it. But be that as it may, if you are determined that the place should remain a private home, we could always sell to a venture capitalist or one of those Internet wallahs? It's people like that who have all the money these days and we'd be sure to get a very good price. We could always keep one of the farms to live in, and of course the stable block. Just think – we would actually be financially solvent for the first time in our lives!"

"Are you mad, woman?! That would be worse still. The poor old house would be smothered in swathes of chintz before you could count up to ten. Goodness knows, they might even install central heating and comfortable furniture! Whatever next? No, no, no, we're not selling to anybody… Sometimes, I admit, even I have been tempted by the idea of selling up, but then I look at that portrait over the fireplace of old Sir Willoughby Cathcart and his young wife with their two children and it reminds me of the duty to my ancestors – a duty to preserve the estate passed down to us through the centuries for the benefit of future generations… and… and…"

Lady Cathcart, fearing that her husband was plunging into one of his sentimental moods, thought it best to intervene before he could continue.

"Do you know," she said, "who that young lady reminds me of?"

"What young lady?"

"The lady in the portrait."

"Well, who does she remind you of, then?"

"Why, Sandra, of course."

Sir Arthur got up from the table to peer more closely at the portrait.

"By God, you're absolutely right, Edith! Amazing! A spitting image. How clever of you to notice."

Sandra and Adam got up to take a closer look. Yes, Adam agreed, there was a certain resemblance.

"What was her name?" Sandra asked.

"Emma, though nothing much is known about her before she married Sir Willoughby other than the fact that her sister was married to a local clergyman."

"When was the portrait painted?" Adam asked.

"Oh… about 1805, I think. They were married around the year 1800. Sir Willoughby was much older than she was, as indeed you can see from the picture. Emma looks so very young and beautiful, doesn't she?"

"Just like Sandra," Lady Cathcart added, smiling fondly at the young lady she expected to become her daughter-in-law.

"There you are, Sandra, my dear," Sir Arthur beamed. "You see you're almost one of the family already!"

Sandra blushed a deep crimson, but she had never felt so happy in all her young life.

Thursday 10th February 2005

Hugo arrived early at Beacon Court to find Gina, who had taken the afternoon off from work, in a state of some agitation. She was due to depart the following morning to spend a rare weekend with her husband in Wilmslow.

"I wish I didn't have to go," she said.

"Well, so do I, but we have to keep Frank happy, don't we?"

"Yes, of course, but you don't actually have to do the 'keeping happy' bit, do you?"

"No, and I confess I can't bear to think about it, you with that brute… rather like the girl with King Kong in the film. Come on, Gina, let's go and cheer each other up"

"Hugo, darling," Gina implored, after the cheering up process in the bedroom had fully run its course, "couldn't you stay on this evening? Make some excuse to Lisa."

"Wish I could, but I've got to go to a meeting of the Sheridan Club."

"The Sheridan Club? What's that? It's not your usual club, is it?"

"No, it's a club devoted to the discussion of politics, the arts, culture, things like that."

"Ooh, I'll bet it is!"

Humming to himself the 'Catalogue Aria' from Don Giovanni, Hugo made his way home, stopping off briefly at the dry-cleaners for the suit he was planning to wear for the evening's event, and at the florists to buy a carnation for his buttonhole.

In essence, Gina was right to be sceptical about the Sheridan Club, which took its name from the restaurant where the meetings took place about four times a year. Nobody took it too seriously. Why would you want to indulge in some deep philosophical debate about politics or art after a long day's toil in the City? Nobody was terribly interested in the background to the latest political crisis, even though one of their members happened to be a well-known political columnist. They'd much prefer to hear about the latest scandal to hit the Westminster village; which 'happily married' government minister, for example, had been caught out having an affair with a nubile young research assistant; which senior party figure had got dead drunk at some international conference, a trip no doubt funded by the long-suffering taxpayer, and wound up dressed in a frock at a transvestite bar in Amsterdam?

Nobody really wanted to listen much to the views of some senior investment banker or stock market analyst on the state of the UK economy or the strength or weakness of the bond market. They would much rather hear the latest crop of smutty jokes doing the rounds of the City dealing rooms.

They might be mildly interested in Hugo's critique of the latest ENO production of The Barber of Seville, but not if he went on for too long about it.

There was, though, an agenda of sorts for each meeting, if only as a justification for the Club's existence going beyond being simply an excuse to eat and drink too much and have a good time. The main item customarily involved a debate upon some topic chosen by the Chairman, usually of a fairly light-hearted nature.

The chosen subject for debate that evening was 'Style, Taste and Fashion – what is the difference and does it matter?'

Almost immediately after the Chairman had spoken a few introductory words, a heated argument began about motor cars.

Which was the Real Man's top choice of car and which particular model in the range?

Which makes of car automatically conferred on its owner the right to be treated as a serious player?

Which car, on the other hand, was now regarded as totally passé, and most liable to damage your street cred?

It was amazing, in fact, how often cars featured in discussions at Sheridan Club meetings, whatever the chosen topic.

The chairman did his best to steer members away from their choice of motor vehicle.

"What about celebrities, culture, cities, clothes, people, modern life?" he asked, hoping to throw the matter open to more general discussion.

The overall view of the members was that hardly anyone had any style these days, especially people in public life and so-called celebrities. Good taste, too, was much in decline.

In fact, "good taste", as one member put it, "had almost become unfashionable". Certainly, fashion today was frequently neither stylish, nor in good taste. All but a few of the younger members murmured agreement with this gloomy assessment of the contemporary scene

The club's slightly foppish wine expert, Ambrose de Courcey, endeavouring to distinguish between taste and style, put forward the view that wine might provide a helpful analogy. Burgundy, he suggested, represented good taste, while champagne had style.

"Style, my dear friends, is all a matter of bubbles."

Before Ambrose could expand upon his theory and explain why it is that the better champagnes produce more but smaller bubbles than the cheaper ones, Hugo caught the Chairman's eye.

"May I say a few words, Mr. Chairman?" "But of course, dear boy."

Hugo, as he was well aware, was expected to play the part of the court jester on these evenings. With this in mind, he always took the trouble to dress a little flamboyantly. He liked, in any case, to distinguish himself from the pinstripe brigade to which most of the other members, almost all of whom worked in the City, belonged. That evening he had chosen to wear with his suit a quite outrageous multi-coloured waistcoat.

Everyone waited in eager anticipation for what Hugo had to say. It would generally be something mildly controversial intended to ginger things up. The members liked that.

"Style may occasionally doff its cap in the direction of taste, and fashion may choose to go where style leads, but they are not the same things," he said. "Now, you see this waistcoat of mine?"

"How could we miss it!" the Chairman intervened. "I noticed a few young chaps wearing something like it at my niece's wedding recently, but nothing quite… quite… so dazzling."

"Well, my fiancée is embarrassed whenever I wear it and considers it in very poor taste, but the other woman in my life, on the other hand, regards it as incredibly stylish, and indeed quite fashionable."

"Which of them is right, then?" a member called Gilbert, always a bit of a stirrer, asked.

"Both of them, probably!" Hugo replied.

"Both of them?!"

"Yes. You see, in my opinion, style, taste and fashion perform quite distinct social functions, although they may of course often overlap.

"Good taste requires an element of restraint involving conformity with an unwritten code which chaps like us are traditionally supposed to understand and observe. Style, however, is all about being individual, standing out from the crowd. Style is about setting a trend; fashion is about following one. You either have style or you don't. One cannot formulate a precise definition, but if you have it, you can often get away with something quite outrageous which defies both present fashion and whatever we may currently regard as good taste – something like my waistcoat, in fact!"

"Jolly good, Hugo!" the Chairman said, pleased that at last someone had brought a little focus to the debate which had seemed in danger of meandering around and losing its way.

Indeed, everyone seemed to consider that Hugo had summed the whole matter up rather neatly. There was really little more to be said.

"Do you mean to say that you maintain a lady on the side, in addition to a fiancée, Hugo?" Gilbert asked. "I must say that's most enterprising of you. I suppose you would say that it shows a certain style, though some might say that it was in rather poor taste of you to mention it!"

"Oh, I'm afraid I have to admit, Gilbert, I was only joking."

"So, nobody really said that your waistcoat was stylish and fashionable, then?!"

"Oh, yes, they did. That was the stepmother of my bride to be."

"I'm very relieved to hear that you were only joking, Hugo, as always, and that you are of course entirely faithful to your charming fiancée," the Chairman said, with a smile of relief. "And now, unless anyone else has anything to add, I think that we may move on to the next item on our agenda. Ambrose is going to talk to us, I believe, about some interesting new wines from the Piedmont region of Italy…"

♪

Later, after the evening at the Sheridan Club had drawn to a close, Hugo and Archie went on to a favourite late-night drinking haunt for a final nightcap.

"Taking a bit of a risk, weren't you, Hugo?"

"What do you mean?"

"Mentioning your other woman or whatever you called her, and you even said who she was. God, what if your affair with Gina comes out into the open? You're finished. No marriage to Lisa, no extravagant lifestyle, no money. You'd have to work for a living."

"I said it was all a joke, didn't I? Besides, it won't come out… not a chance."

"Well, I don't know about that…"

"Of course, it won't. And even if it did, nobody would ever believe it anyway. It's too outrageous to be true!"

"Yes, but it is true, isn't it?"

"You obviously weren't listening to me back there at Sheridan's, Archie. If you're outrageous enough, you can get away with anything."

"But that was in a slightly different context, Hugo."

"Not really. The principle is much the same."

"Lack of principle, I'd call it!"

"Oh, very droll, Archie."

"Well, all I can say is that nobody gets away with riding two horses like you are doing indefinitely. Someday you'll fall off, and not just off one horse, mind you, but both of them!"

Thursday 17th March 2005

"Where's the Weetabix, then?"

"I don't think there is any… I think Jane had the last one in the packet before she went off this morning."

"Oh God!" Gerald Higginbottom stopped rummaging in the cupboard, and looked round despairingly at his wife, Moira, who was sitting at the kitchen table nursing a cup of coffee.

"Don't worry, I'm going to the supermarket today. I'll get some more. It's not the end of the world, you know."

"Well, it is for me. I'm bloody constipated again. Weetabix is the only thing which does the trick… No, on reflection, I agree it's not actually the end of the world. In fact, the world is stuck up there unable to come to an end."

"Oh really, Gerald, that's disgusting! Why must you say these things at breakfast? Anyway, what are you doing today, anything special?"

"No, not really. I've got a partners' meeting this morning which I'm not looking forward to."

"But I thought you only had partners' meetings on the first Monday of the month."

"Normally, yes, but this is a special meeting to consider certain advice from Louther & Tomkins, our PR people, including, I have to tell you, changing the firm's name."

"Changing the name? But what's wrong with Glade Higginbottom & Associates? It sounds eminently respectable."

"Not snappy enough apparently. Old-fashioned respectability is not, I'm told, where it's at these days. The younger partners want to drop Higginbottom. 'Too, like, uncool', as our daughter might put it."

"You mean they want to kick you out."

"No, no. Just the name. They want to drop the name Higginbottom from the firm's name."

"But, but… they can't."

"Oh yes they can."

"Well, what do these young tykes propose that the firm is called, then?"

"Just 'Glades'."

"Ridiculous! It sounds like that old people's home in Esher where they sent poor old Auntie Audrey."

"Indeed. Or, worse still, perhaps a name for a seedy nightclub!"

"Well, there you are then. Scarcely suitable for a well-established firm of architects specializing in the conversion of Georgian and Victorian buildings, surely?"

"It's not worth me making a fuss, dear. Besides, after our merger with Tom Glade's outfit the firm has done lots of whizzo new stuff along the M4 corridor – business parks, distribution centres, out of town stores, that sort of thing. They want to project a more up-to-date image."

"You mark my words, Gerald, you let them drop your name and they'll be dropping you next."

Before he could think of anything to say next, the telephone rang in the hall.

"Please may I speak to Mr. Higginbottom?"

"Speaking."

"Hello, this is Dave here, Dave Riley. I'm sorry to phone you at home, but I wanted to catch you early before you got too tied up. I tried to contact you yesterday at the office, but you'd already left."

For a moment he was at a loss. The world seemed to be full of Daves, especially in the building trade. Fortunately, he remembered who it was this time. This Dave Riley chap was the project manager of an office conversion project near the British Museum for intended occupation by a firm of insurance brokers as their headquarters. Gerald's firm had been retained as architects.

"That's all right, Dave. What can I do for you?"

"There's a bit of a problem at number 46. We've found quite a large area of damp in the two larger rooms on the top floor. I don't know where it's coming from and I couldn't find any obvious cause for it. I'm worried that it might significantly hold up the next phase of the works if it turns out to be something major. As you know we are working to a very tight timescale as the clients want to take possession in three months' time."

"Well, I'd better come and take a look. I should be with you within the hour."

Normally speaking a problem necessitating an urgent unscheduled site visit was a damn nuisance. It led to considerable disruption of the working day. In this case, however, he was very pleased to have an excuse not to attend the partners' meeting.

Meetings used to be entertaining gatherings in the old days but since the merger a different ethos prevailed. Gin and jokes had given way to a regime of mirthless formality and bottled water. No fun at all.

On the way to the tube station, Gerald phoned the office on his mobile. He asked to speak to Malcolm Dobson, the newly appointed partnership secretary. Malcolm was an eager young man whose extraordinary, if rather irritating, enthusiasm made him ideally suited to the role. The trouble was that he was one of that new breed of funless functionaries so common these days, and Gerald found it very hard not to make fun of him. Poor Malcolm, being a little light in the humour department, took everything at face value which, of course, made making fun of him all the more enjoyable. Malcolm was unavailable to speak when the call came through but Gerald was invited to leave a message on the voicemail. This suited his purpose admirably. He could say what he liked without being interrupted.

"Hello, Malcolm," he said, "this is Gerald. I'm sorry that I won't be able to attend the partners' meeting this morning. An urgent problem has cropped up and I have to go on site. I regret I didn't quite finish reading the PR people's report… a bit indigestible as usual with all that vulgar ungrammatical business jargon, nouns pretending to be verbs and vice versa… I'm happy, however, to leave it to the other partners to make the right decisions on all matters – apart from, that is, the proposal to change the name of the firm. I do have some reservations there which perhaps you would kindly convey to the meeting on my behalf.

"Moira thinks that Glades sounds like the name of an old folk's home, while I thought it could well be a name for a nightclub. Either way, surely it doesn't send out quite the right signal to the punters.

"I suspect, if we are all honest about it, it's my bottom where the problem really lies. Of course, I know we must never forget the bottom line, but the fact is that 'anal' has now become a pejorative term. All the young use it these days to describe things they don't like. The solution is simple – let the 'bottom' fall out of my name! Let us be known in future as 'Higgins Glade'. I do hope this idea commends itself to everyone as a satisfactory compromise. Hope to see you later."

Feeling more than usually pleased with himself, Gerald arrived at the property in Bloomsbury to find an anxious young project manager waiting for him. They climbed together to the top of the building to look at the problem.

Certainly, there was some damp there. It looked to be of recent origin rather than something long-standing. Opening a window, he clambered out onto the scaffolding and, via a ladder, made his way up to the roof above. The cause of the damp soon became apparent. There was a loose coping stone on top of the parapet wall which was leaning at a slight angle and letting the rainwater run in underneath. It had probably become dislodged accidentally when the contractors were up on the roof renewing the old flashings and re-pointing the brickwork. Not much of a problem really and easy to remedy. He returned to the top storey of the building again by the same route and climbed back through the window with a helping hand from Dave Riley, who had waited for him while he carried out his inspection. He told him what he had discovered and asked him to go and find the building foreman so that he could explain to him what needed to be done.

As he waited for the foreman to come up, he used the opportunity for a quick inspection. It was some time ago since he had been up on this floor and the contractors were only just making a start on this part of the building. Their first job was to dismantle most of the interior non-load-bearing walls and this work had already commenced. There was a fair amount of rubble already. He noticed in one corner a dusty pile of old papers and documents. Material often got tucked away for years behind walls, partitions, false ceilings and in other dark and inaccessible places. It was extraordinary what came to light when major refurbishment works were done, particularly in the case of an old house like this one.

Only a week or so before he had come across a copy of the *Times* published on the first day of the general strike in 1926, and he always took a keen interest in these things.

Walking over, he stooped down to take a closer look at the pile, which was more substantial than he had first thought.

Among the miscellaneous junk, he found some newspapers from the 1960s and 70s, but there was also some really old stuff – a railway timetable from 1845 and a theatre programme for the first production of 'Lady Windermere's Fan' in 1892. It was then that he noticed a separate large bundle of papers right at the bottom of the pile which was loosely held together with some badly degraded pink ribbon. Gingerly he extracted this bundle from the rest of the pile. The pink ribbon fell apart almost immediately and Gerald just managed to avoid dropping the whole thing on the floor. He took it to the window where he could see better in the light and, resting it on the wide sill, started to thumb through.

The bundle was effectively in two parts: one consisted of a musical score, while the other comprised page upon page of writing in German, including many sections inset which he guessed might be the words for songs or arias. Plainly it had suffered some damage from damp mould, and parts were a bit indistinct, but overall, on a brief perusal, most of it seemed legible enough. In the score, there were words in German written between the lines of music and also things like Arie and Chor written above sections of the music. One did not have to be a genius to conclude that the musical part of the manuscript must be the score of some choral work, perhaps an opera, while the written part would be – what was it called, now? Oh yes, the libretto. There was nothing to indicate who had written either the music or the libretto, and possibly there was a title page missing. This thing might be of some importance, Gerald thought, and he decided that he had better take it away with him.

It was as well that he had come on the scene when he did. Half an hour later the contractors' men had completely cleared the area. The manuscript would certainly have been thrown into the chute attached to the scaffolding, along with all the rest of the rubble and detritus, whence it would have pirouetted its way down into the skip in the street below, never to be seen again.

Wednesday 23rd March 2005

"Do you know you've got a lovely little bottom?"

Hugo Belcher followed Lisa as she made her way into the kitchen. Moving up close behind her as she stood by the coffee-maker, he gently patted her bottom, before encircling her with his arms and drawing her body towards him. Lisa lent backwards slightly, turning her head around to give him a kiss on the cheek.

"In fact," Hugo continued, "it was your bottom that first attracted me. It was sitting there, I recall, in its smart little navy-blue trouser suit on a stool at the bar of Chez Véronique, looking absolutely scrumptious."

"It wasn't my beautiful eyes, then?"

"No, no, it was definitely the bottom. I hadn't met you then of course. You were with that tall fellow with strange popping-out eyes and a large Adam's apple."

"You mean Derek Waltham, my pension advisor – and not at all as ugly as you make him out. Such a nice, kind man, too. Now, there's a true British gentleman for you."

"English gentleman, you mean. There's no such thing as a British gentleman."

"But what about the Scots, the Irish, and the Welsh – can't they be gentlemen too?"

"Of course not. If any of our Celtic brethren wishes to masquerade as a gentleman, he simply must pretend to be English."

"But, what about Daddy? He's Italian by birth."

"Well, your father has lived here since he was a boy… in fact, come to think of it, the Romans were here for centuries. Perhaps the Italians, as their descendants, can be treated as honorary gentlemen – and certainly, I must concede, this applies to your dear father."

What balderdash I speak, Hugo thought to himself. Of course, race was irrelevant, but gentlemen are generally polite, charming, considerate souls from wherever they come. Frank was about as boorish, self-seeking and ruthless as it is possible for a chap to be – hardly very gentlemanly characteristics. Of course, he could be polite and was even capable of exercising a certain persuasive charm if he felt that this would be a surer route to getting his way than his preferred method of bullying the shit out of some poor sod, but politeness and charm were to him simply a cloak, like a mantle of snow upon a bleak mountainside only just covering the jagged rocks and hideous chasms beneath. The only area of tender care and consideration in his icy, calculating heart was exclusively reserved for his daughter and only child, Lisa, to whom Hugo was now engaged.

Hugo was not being entirely insincere when he talked about Lisa's posterior. It was indeed a nice, neat little bottom; by far her best feature, in fact. There was, though, no shortage of nice little bottoms in the world, and he had in his time patted a great many of them, but not ones which came attached to a nice large inheritance, as Lisa's did.

Lisa hurriedly nibbled a piece of dry toast and in two quick gulps drained her cup of coffee.

"Look at the time!" she said. "I must get going, or I'll be late for work again."

"I hardly think they're going to sack you, darling."

"That's not the point," Lisa answered primly. She resented the implication behind Hugo's teasing remark. "See you this evening – and remember the Martins are coming for drinks at six – and… oh, Hugo," she said, her tone softening, "I love you. I love you very, very much."

"And I love you too, my dear." He replied, standing up to kiss her goodbye.

Bugger the Martins! Hugo thought, as Lisa closed the front door behind her. Another tedious evening with a tedious couple with whom he had absolutely nothing in common. Jill Martin worked with Lisa and was one of the few rather less posh of her colleagues. Her husband, Garry, was a graphic designer at an advertising agency. Hugo found Garry a profoundly irritating young man, especially his annoying habit of finding some reason for disagreeing with almost everything Hugo had to say, even things which one might have thought were not particularly controversial. Every time he caught Jill's eye, she gave him a hostile sort of look. Plainly she didn't like him very much and, though he had no very good reason for thinking so, he had an uncomfortable feeling that she was suspicious of his motives in relation to Lisa, her friend.

With a sigh, he resumed his seat, picked up the morning newspaper and idly turned the pages as he sipped his coffee.

There had been a meeting the day before in Brussels of European agriculture ministers to discuss new proposals by the

European Commission for regulating the manufacture of cheese and dairy products. The meeting had become increasingly acrimonious, and at one point, the Italian representative had expressed the view that Dutch cheese was completely devoid of taste, whereupon the entire Dutch delegation had walked out, bringing the discussions to a premature close. Later an official communiqué reported that substantial progress had been made.

A strike of French air traffic controllers threatened widespread delays to many flights.

Yet another public library, this time somewhere in South London, had banned Pinocchio story books on the grounds that the elongation of Pinocchio's nose might be upsetting to children with facial deformities. A ban on Pinocchio in local schools was under consideration for similar reasons.

There had been extensive flooding in North Wales.

The latest Middle East peace initiative had collapsed amidst a flurry of recriminations.

A genetically modified carrot had grown to a size of eighteen inches.

Altogether, a pretty average sort of news day, he thought, until an article in the home news section caught his attention:

OPERA MANUSCRIPT FOUND

The manuscript of a German opera score complete with libretto, believed to be more than 200 years old, has been found during the course of conversion works to a property in Bloomsbury near the British Museum. It is not certain to whom the opera can be attributed. Some pages are illegible as a result of damage by mould and a few, including the title page, appear to be missing, but the score and libretto seem otherwise complete and in good condition. A spokesman for the Royal Academy of Music described the discovery as "potentially very significant". Arrangements have been made for the manuscript and libretto to be examined by eminent musicologist, Professor Justin Wetherby.

Well, well, Hugo thought, that sounds most interesting… I must keep tabs on this one.

Monday 4th April 2005

A taxi drew up outside the Royal Academy of Music, out of which stepped a dapper old gentleman sporting a well-trimmed grey beard, a smart brown trilby and a beautifully tailored suit in a pattern of Prince-of-Wales check. Professor Justin Wetherby had arrived to examine the opera score and libretto recently discovered in Bloomsbury. The Academy was considered a good place for Wetherby to conduct his researches and the score and libretto would be kept there in the interests of security.

As the architect who found it had noticed, some pages of the manuscript had been lost or were partially indecipherable as a result of mould, but the rest was in a pretty fair condition. The lost pages of the score comprised the first part of the overture, which would, Wetherby presumed, have included the title of the work, and also part of the finale. In addition to the absence of any title, there was no indication of the name either of the composer or of the librettist, or indeed of the story or play upon which the libretto and opera were based. Presumably all or most of this information would have appeared in the missing title page. The libretto, which was not in the same hand as the musical score, seemed to be complete. The title page was there but had been so severely affected by mould as to be unreadable. It was clear that the opera was based on the libretto – both were in German and, at least upon a cursory examination, the words of arias, duets and so forth which appeared in the opera score exactly or very closely reflected those in the libretto.

Refusing an offer of coffee, he got down to work at once. He had decided that the best approach would be to examine the libretto first before beginning a detailed analysis of the music. He spoke and read German well so this presented no problem.

He began to read.

The early scenes seemed vaguely familiar to Wetherby, but he couldn't quite place them at first. The libretto, for the most part, provided good settings for the music, but he had a curious feeling that the work on which it was based was originally in some other language; Italian, possibly, as it was set in Venice. He read on, trying to discern the gist of the typically convoluted plot.

Suddenly, Wetherby's vague memory shifted into focus. He was right – the original was indeed Italian, and he now realised where the libretto had come from. It was based on Carlo Goldoni's famous comic play The Servant of Two Masters – Il Servitore di Due Padroni.

He continued reading to remind himself of the entire plot and all the subplots.

Basically, though, glossing over the complications of the plot and subplots, the central character is Truffaldino, the servant of the play's title. He, unbeknown to his employer (incidentally, a woman disguised as a man), takes up simultaneous employment with a second employer in order to double his income. The second employer just happens to be his first employer's former lover. Truffaldino also falls in love with a certain lady's maid called Smeraldina.

There are further twists and imbroglios, often due to the confusion which arises from Truffaldino's dual employment, but in the end all the plots are finally resolved.

The proposed marriage between Truffaldino and Smeraldina, however, is opposed because it seems that Smeraldina is already betrothed to another servant.

Truffaldino has no alternative but to admit that this other servant is none other than himself and that he is in fact... the servant of two masters!

Having familiarised himself sufficiently with the libretto, Wetherby began a methodical study of the music itself; first the overture and then scene by scene. Staying at his London club during the week and returning home to Wiltshire at weekends, it took him almost three weeks to complete his preliminary examination of the score, and the more he studied it, the more amazed he became. Part of the overture was, of course, missing, but from what remained, it was clearly a most spirited and imaginative piece. In particular, he noted, there were some fine passages for the woodwind instruments.

Indeed, the overture was just a foretaste of what was to come. As Wetherby read on through the score, he could barely contain his astonishment. The quality of the music was really quite outstanding. Each scene brought some new wonder.

Truffaldino's aria at his first buffoonish appearance is a masterpiece of comic humour, complete with a splendidly witty solo for bassoon providing an admirable accompaniment to the voice part.

Later in the first act, Truffaldino and Smeraldina sing a beautiful, tenderly amusing love duet, accompanied only by muted strings.

In the next act, there is a wonderfully raucous banquet scene with full orchestra and chorus.

The final scene of the last act culminates in a marvellous aria for Truffaldino in which he is forced to make the famous admission upon which the title of Goldoni's play, and presumably that of the opera, was based.

There were, in fact, many arias, duets and ensembles in each of the acts of equal brilliance and it would be true to say that there was not one single moment of weak invention in the entire work. Wetherby considered, too, that it ought to be fairly easy to make an adequate reconstruction of all the missing or illegible parts of the score for performance purposes.

This was beginning to look, he thought, like one of the most exciting musical discoveries for a century.

Thursday 21st April 2005

As Professor Wetherby returned to his club for the evening, towards the end of the period in which he had studied the score, a conclusion was beginning to form in his mind, a conclusion which would give rise to great excitement in the world of opera and beyond – not to mention a tidal wave of scholarly controversy.

At about the same time as Wetherby pensively sipped a gin and tonic in the club bar, Hugo and Gina were sipping champagne together in bed in a lull between their own torrid duets. If music be the food of love, then champagne must be the liquid refreshment, Hugo thought, as he reached over for the bottle to pour himself another glass.

In fact, Hugo should by rights that evening have been appreciating real music: a concert of string quartets by Haydn and Schubert at the Wigmore Hall, which he was due to review for the arts supplement of one of the Sunday papers. That was where poor Lisa thought he was at this very moment. He had arranged, however, for one of his more reliable and musically knowledgeable chums to be in attendance, who would provide him in the morning with a full account of the performance upon which to base his review.

"Pity we seem to have run out of the company's supply of the Dom Pérignon. A decent champagne is essential to my well-being, you know. You really should have a word with Frank's office, Gina, get them to stock the place up again properly. Some wretched minion deserves a bit of a bollocking, in my view. Very remiss, very remiss indeed… Still, I have to say this stuff you bought today is a most acceptable alternative."

"So I should think. It wasn't that cheap, you know! And while you're about it, what about a top up for me too, please?"

Just as he was replenishing Gina's glass, they both heard the faint but quite discernible sound of a key being turned in a lock – the lock to the front door of the apartment. No doubt about it.

"Christ! Who's that?" Hugo spluttered.

"Jesus! It must be Frank – he's the only other one with a key, one of his flying visits. Quick, quick into the bathroom! Go, go!"

Hugo reacted like a nervous gazelle at the first scent of a stalking leopard. It was not the first occasion on which he had found himself in a similar position. He jumped out of the bed, and scooping up his clothes on the way under one arm, legged it to the bathroom in less than five seconds flat, still clutching the glass of champagne in his free hand.

Fortunately, Frank made his way first to the drawing room. Finding no one there he retreated to the hallway.

"Anybody home?" he called out.

"Yes, I'm in here."

Frank made his way to the master bedroom.

"Christ, you're in bed!"

"How clever of you to notice, Frank!"

"Bit early, isn't it?"

"Well, I was tired…"

"And drinking champagne too…"

"And why not, for heaven's sake? I had a very busy day at the gallery…What brings you to London, by the way? You never told me you were coming, or I'd have smartened the place up a bit."

"Had to come down for a meeting with our auditors today."

"Oh, I see."

"Don't know why they always have to make a fucking meal of things. Some bloody crap about capital allowances…"

"Frank."

"Yes, Amore."

"Come to bed!"

"Eh?"

"Come to bed with me, for fuck's sake!"

"Si, si, yeah, sure, sure… but I think I'll just take a quick shower – been in some fuckin' city office without any fuckin' windows all fuckin' day, need to freshen up—"

"No, no, Frank! I can't wait – I want you now!"

With this, Gina threw back the duvet to reveal herself in all her nakedness.

Not even the primmest preacher of the most sternly Baptist chapel in deepest mid-Wales could have resisted such an invitation, and Frank, wide- eyed, took off his jacket, threw it over a chair, unzipped his trousers and leapt onto the bed without even troubling to remove his tie or his stylish Italian shoes. With Frank occupied, Hugo stealthily, now more or less fully clothed, crept from the bathroom, tucking his shirt into his trousers as he went. Still with his glass of champagne in hand, he tiptoed quietly the short distance to the bedroom door and made good his escape.

When Frank's urges had been more than amply satisfied, he clambered off the bed to go and take his long-awaited shower. Gina, breathing a deep sigh of relief, sat up in bed to reach for her gown. It was then to her horror that she noticed something coiled like a snake on the floor.

It was Hugo's Old Etonian tie. He must have dropped it on the way out, curse him. Keeping an eye on the bathroom door, she swung herself out of bed, stooped to pick it up and hurriedly bundled it into the drawer in her dressing table where she kept her underwear.

It had been as damn a close-run fucking thing as Waterloo!

Friday 22nd April 2005

"Do you know what?"

"No, what?"

"By the way, isn't it odd?" Adam said. "The way, I mean, in which we often start a conversation like that. I've just said, 'Do you know what?' and of course you couldn't possibly know, so you reply, just as you did then, 'No, what?' It's a complete waste of breath when you think about it, yet somehow, we all still resort to these odd verbal formulations. Perhaps I shall write a book entitled 'Meaningless Conversational Devices in Daily Use' or something of the sort. It would make a jolly good stocking filler at Christmas, don't you think?"

"Adam, for God's sake, what is it you want to tell me?" Sandra asked, exasperated.

"Do you know, I've quite forgotten."

"Oh, Adam!"

"No, no, it's all right, I remember now. I went out to lunch today with one of our authors… guess where, incidentally?"

"That's almost as bad as 'Do you know what?' Come on, tell me. Where?"

"Chez Véronique."

"You bastard! Why wasn't I, like, invited?"

"Well, I didn't know where he was going to take me until the last moment. It was at his invitation, you see."

"Yes, I'll bet. Is that what you wanted to tell me, then, to torment me with stories of all the, like, fabulous food and wine you had?"

"No, no, not at all. You see there was this friend of his there, whom he had also invited to lunch – a most distinguished man. Well, I had quite a long chat with him, this distinguished chap. I said that you were a singer, interested in opera and all that, and I mentioned your concert in Hammersmith next month…"

"Oh, yes?"

"Well, he said he'd love to come and hear you sing. Luckily he's free on that evening."

"I see… and that's it, is it? That's what you like wanted to tell me?"

"Yes."

"Well, I'll send him a ticket, then."

"Look, Sandra, I don't think you quite appreciate the significance of what I'm trying to say to you. This chap's a famous conductor, and much in demand the world over. If he thinks you're any good – and he certainly will, we can be sure of that – well, it could be the beginning of something… the breakthrough you've always been looking for. His name is Marcus Lismore, Sir Marcus Lismore. You may know of him, perhaps?"

"Yeah, I do. …My music teacher has lent me some CDs…says he's a really great conductor. Oh, Adam, this is fantastic! Amazing!" she said, throwing her arms around him. "You should go to Chez Véronique more often. Only next time, promise, like, you'll take me too!"

Tuesday 26th April 2005

Not long after Frank Belcanto's unexpected and near disastrous intrusion, Hugo sat at his desk, laptop open before him, endeavouring to complete a review of a recent performance of

Bellini's famous opera 'Norma'.

Hugo enjoyed his work as a music critic and journalist, in fact even more now that it had become essentially a hobby rather than a job upon which his livelihood depended. It irked him though that his peers didn't really take him seriously, let alone treat him as an equal. He had, among other musical accomplishments, obtained a Master's degree in the History of Western Music and felt quite as qualified to do the job as they were. Further, he had a knack of spotting new musical talent, and fancied that he wrote better than most of them. Of course, the trouble was that other pleasures often intervened and took precedence over what he should have been doing, and, since his student days, he had become lazy too, preferring a shortcut, a fudge, or an intelligent guess to the rigorous research often required.

His reviews, however, were invariably witty, entertaining pieces, if not as erudite sometimes as they ought to have been. Normally he had little difficulty in stringing something together, but this review had frankly been a bit of a struggle, largely due to the fact that he had had another of those lengthy lunches with chums at his club, from which he had not sufficiently recovered by the time the curtain went up. As a result, he had nodded off to sleep at crucial moments of the performance and had failed to make any notes.

After much pondering, a brilliant idea occurred to him. He would adapt a review of another performance of Norma that he had written a couple of years ago for a different newspaper, and meld with it extracts from a short piece he had written for a monthly classical music magazine about a new CD box set of Rigoletto, which happily included three singers from the current cast of Norma. Provided he confined himself to writing about the talents of the singers whilst avoiding mention of the arias they were actually singing, he felt sure nobody would notice.

Relieved at finding a solution to what had seemed only a few moments before to be an insuperable problem, he set to work with renewed vigour. It didn't take long to polish the thing off and e-mail it to the editor concerned, and, after visiting the fridge and pouring himself a beer, he settled himself comfortably in his favourite chair and turned on the television to catch the last of the early evening news.

"…collapse today of talks with the trade unions in Paris, the further strike by French air traffic controllers scheduled for this weekend looks now certain to go ahead. This will be the third such strike in six weeks, and there is still no sign of an end to the dispute.

"The government today announced the appointment of a taskforce charged with rolling out a programme to deal with the invasion of jellyfish which experts predict will affect our coastal waters as a result of the anticipated rise in sea temperatures caused by global warming."

A picture appeared on the screen of some appropriately earnest-looking boffin prodding with a stick some nasty-looking blob-like objects washed up on a windswept strand somewhere on the north Devon coast.

"And, finally tonight," the newsreader continued, "an item which is certain to be of great interest to music lovers the world over. The manuscript of the opera, reported recently to have been found during the course of refurbishment works at a property near the British Museum, may have been composed by none other than Wolfgang Amadeus Mozart. This is the view, at least, of Professor Justin Wetherby, the musicologist who was asked to examine it, and whom we are fortunate to have with us here in the studio today.

"Good evening, Professor Wetherby." "Good evening."

"So, you really consider this may be a lost work by Mozart?"

"Well, first of all, may I say that we are only now at a very preliminary stage. I have just completed my initial examination of the score. There are many further investigations to be undertaken…"

"Quite, quite, Professor, but this is your initial view – your gut feeling, if I may put it that way?"

"Yes. That is indeed my opinion."

"But on what do you base this view? I mean, what evidence is there?"

"We know from a letter to his father, Leopold, that Mozart had started to compose an opera in German based on a play entitled The Servant of Two Masters by the Italian playwright Carlo Goldoni. The manuscript which has been discovered is a German opera based on this very same play. It is my firm belief that the score of Mozart's lost opera The Servant of Two Masters, or at least a copy of it, has at last come to light. It would be too much to believe that this is simply a coincidence."

"But the score is presumably not in Mozart's own hand, is it?"

"No, it isn't. If the manuscript had been in Mozart's own hand that would of course have put the matter beyond doubt, but the fact that it isn't does not, of course, invalidate my opinion in any way. This manuscript, I mean the one which has been found, is most probably a copy prepared by another musician or a professional copyist – possibly in preparation for a performance or as a fair copy for submission to publishers or for some other reason.

'It is not unusual for the only extant source of a musical work to be either a printed score or a manuscript in a hand other than that of the actual composer.

'We certainly don't have original autograph scores for many works, even some which are very famous. My opinion that the work is by Mozart is based also, I might say, on the music itself, which is absolutely remarkable. It achieves a perfection of which I do not think any other composer would have been capable. If I'm right, this will certainly be the most important musical discovery in decades."

"But why should it have turned up in an attic here in London?"

"There could be any number of reasons, and we may never know the answer. It would be fruitless at this stage to speculate. Just like valuable paintings, however, lost musical scores often come to light in the most unlikely of places."

"Well, I'm sure that we shall be hearing much more about this interesting discovery in the months to come. Thank you very much, Professor Wetherby, for coming here this evening to talk to us."

"It was my pleasure."

"Viewers who are interested may like to tune into BBC Radio 4 on the evening of the 4th of May, when Professor Wetherby will be joining a panel of distinguished experts to discuss the recently found score in greater depth. That's Wednesday the 4th of May at 10.30pm on Radio 4, and the programme is entitled 'Who wrote the Bloomsbury opera?'. Keen opera-goers might also be interested to know that The Royal Opera have already expressed interest in mounting a performance of the opera possibly next year to coincide with the 250th anniversary of Mozart's birth."

Well, well! Hugo thought. Better listen to that!

"Now, for tomorrow's weather, we go to…" Brr-brr, brr-brr, the telephone rang.

Hugo reached for the remote control, turned the set to standby and got up from his chair to answer the call.

It was Gina.

"That you, Hugo?"

"Yes, of course it's me. Who did you think it was – the Emperor of Japan?"

"I mean, Lisa's not there, is she?"

"No, not home from work yet. But what is all this? You don't sound yourself."

"Well, I'm worried, Hugo… I think I'm being spied on."

"Spied on? What on earth do you mean?"

"Well, ever since Frank nearly caught us in the act that day, I've had a kind of uncomfortable feeling, though I can't quite explain it. Then this evening, when I came back from the gallery, there was this man on the corner of the street looking at me, I'm sure he was."

"What man? I mean, what did he look like?"

"Well, he was dark looking…"

"You mean West Indian or African."

"No, more of a Mediterranean type – Spanish, Greek, Italian, something like that…"

"What sort of man was he? I mean, did he appear well-to-do, well- dressed, or what?"

"Oh, no. He was more like a student or something. Hooded tracksuit, trainers – that sort of thing. You know what I mean?"

"Look, Gina, the earth crawls with vile, hooded youth up to no good. He was probably just looking for a chance to mug someone. You've simply got to be on your guard with people like that about. Nothing more to it than that, I'm quite sure."

"You don't think he was spying on me, then… for Frank, I mean?"

"No, of course not. Don't be ridiculous."

"You really don't think so?"

"Of course, I don't."

"Well, perhaps you're right… perhaps I'm overreacting. You always make me feel so much better about things, Hugo. What would I do without you? When are you coming to see me next?"

"Now, let me see, now. Where are we are…Tuesday… Well, I

can't tomorrow. You know that I'm off to Paris with Lisa for a few days on the Eurostar. Tonight, we're meeting with some friends for dinner, but I could come right now for an hour or so. We don't have to go out till eight."

"Oh yes, please, Hugo – do come. I feel I need you now more than ever."

"I'm on the way."

Hugo wrote a swift note for Lisa to say that he had gone out to meet a friend for a quick drink. It took him less than ten minutes to walk the short distance round to Beacon Court.

It was later as he passed by, on his return home, that he too thought he saw someone loitering in the side drive which led to the rear of Beacon Court.

He contemplated going to have a look but swiftly thought better of it. It was probably just the caretaker or nobody of importance, he thought, and if it was someone up to no good, he might get mugged himself … no sense in that.

By the time he reached home, the whole episode had completely passed from his mind.

Wednesday 20th June 1804

It was the same old story – the unexpected arrival on the scene of an adoring husband only to find his beloved spouse in the arms of another man.

The other man in this case was Antonin Vasylicek, or rather Antoine Vascal as he now preferred to call himself since finally deciding to make France his permanent home. The luckless, adoring husband was Maître Eugene Pincheau, a distinguished Parisian lawyer.

Unbeknown to their respective husbands, Amélie Pincheau, wife of Eugene, and her cousin Louise Duboisset had for some time been rivals for Antoine's affections, a rivalry made all the worse by the fact that the two of them had not been on speaking terms for several years following a bitter row over a family inheritance.

Madame Pincheau had managed to persuade her husband to engage Antoine for a more than usually generous fee to give music lessons to her eldest daughter Cécile, but on the strict condition that he must not accept employment at the Duboisset household.

In the same week, Louise Duboisset had pleaded with her husband, Gérard, to offer even more advantageous terms to Antoine to teach the piano to their two young children, Edouard and Evangeline, on the absolute understanding, needless to say, that he would decline the Pincheau appointment.

Naturally Antoine accepted both offers. Neither position would require his full-time attendance, and he ought to be able to fulfil both commitments with ease. The fact that the Pincheau residence and that of the Duboisset family were at opposite ends of the same street in the Marais district would, it was true, pose certain risks, but Antoine, with characteristic insouciance, brushed these aside. If he conducted matters with care, he told himself, there was no reason why his duplicity should be exposed, and furthermore he would thereby double his income.

Madame Pincheau and Madame Duboisset were both most attractive women but quite different in character and appearance. Amélie Pincheau was a short, blonde, coquettish woman, fleshy, feisty and fun, while Louise Duboisset was dark-haired with a tall graceful figure, large soulful eyes and a sensitive disposition. For a man who appreciated variety, Antoine would have found it hard to forsake one for the other. It was not a choice, however, he needed to make, since he was enjoying simultaneous liaisons with both women; liaisons, indeed, which his acceptance of appointments in both households did much to facilitate.

It was all too good to be true, of course. Sooner or later, a dégringolade was inevitable.

One day, Madame Duboisset happened to be passing the servants' parlour where a young housemaid in the employment of the Pincheau family was in conversation with Grégoire, her husband's manservant, with whom she was on terms of some familiarity. There was laughter and the name 'Monsieur Vascal' was mentioned. All ears, Louise Duboisset could not stop herself from eavesdropping. What she overheard caused her beautiful, soulful eyes to flood with tears.

Managing with some effort to compose herself, her eyes, though reddened with tears, quickly lost their soulfulness, acquiring instead a steely glint, and her mood changed to one of cold fury.

Immediately, without troubling the servants to fetch her cloak, Madame Duboisset set forth for the law courts where she anticipated she would find Maître Pincheau.

She found him indeed, without difficulty, surrounded by nervous litigants waiting for their cases to be called.

"That fat trollop of a wife of yours is sleeping with that… that creature Vascal, the music teacher," she blurted out. "I heard it myself from the servants."

Well aware, of course, of the froideur which pervaded relations between Madame Duboisset and his wife, Maître Pincheau was not at first inclined to believe her. What she said seemed to him both insulting and absurd.

"Alors, Monsieur. Are you going to do something about it or are you content to remain un mari trompé, a laughing stock of the whole quartier!?"

Horrible doubts began to invade his naturally suspicious legal mind. Swiftly gathering up his papers, he hurried away, leaving the gaggle of bemused litigants bobbing in his wake. As he arrived home and mounted the stairs, he heard giggles coming from the matrimonial bedroom and the sound of a man's voice. Horrible doubt turned to dreadful certainty. He made a brief detour to his study and took a pistol from a drawer of his desk. Lawyerly discretion had by now entirely deserted him to be replaced by a fierce all-consuming rage.

Ever since the unfortunate incident in Bath, Antoine had taken precautions when conducting liaisons with other men's wives, in case the worst should happen. First, he took care never entirely to remove all his clothing, especially, if possible, to keep his boots on or at least to leave them in an accessible position, in case sudden flight became an urgent priority.

Secondly, he would always ensure that an easy escape route was available. On this occasion, he had adopted the simple expedient of opening a window from which it was but a short leap to the roof of an adjoining building. At the far end of this roof, there was an ancient wisteria conveniently growing up against the end wall, down which one could descend to a rear alleyway running between the backs of the houses and those in the next street.

What Antoine had not bargained for, however, was that the wretched Pincheau would be armed with a pistol. He had managed to escape through the open window just as the fellow had entered the room, and was halfway across the roof when he heard a loud bang. There was no sensation at first and he thought the shot must have gone wide, but then quite suddenly he felt a sharp, searing pain in his left buttock. Gasping in shock, he nearly lost his balance, dislodging several tiles in the process which clattered down the side of the roof and crashed to the ground. Pincheau had managed to reload quickly and another shot ricocheted off a nearby chimney stack before Antoine was able to reach the far gable and very gingerly lower himself down the wisteria to the dark alleyway below.

His poor posterior by now was throbbing like a volcano fit to erupt, but hearing distant footsteps and muffled shouts behind him, he hurried along through the narrow streets of the Marais as fast as his wound would allow. Presently, he found himself close to the Seine, and staggered across the Pont Marie onto the Île Saint-Louis opposite. In the hope of evading his pursuer, he just managed, now almost fainting with pain, to force himself to limp the remaining distance to the Church of St Louis itself, where he took refuge. Once safely inside the ornate baroque interior, he stopped at last to regain his breath, anxiously wondering if he had been seen entering the church. A full five minutes passed and no Pincheau. Thank God, he thought, nodding dutifully in the direction of the altar. Once more, it seemed, he had escaped!

A requiem mass for some local worthy was in progress, and badly needing to rest, he limped painfully to the nearest available place to sit. Breathing a heavy sigh of relief, he sat down, only to shoot to his feet again with a yelp of agony. He could neither sit nor stand without intolerable discomfort. What was he to do? It was the end in more ways than one.

"What is the matter? Are you ill?" a voice asked.

He turned to face the person who had spoken, and found himself staring into a pair of the most bewitchingly beautiful pair of eyes he had ever seen. They were wide and green, and they stared back at him with a mixture of astonishment and amusement in more or less equal measure.

"It is my war wound," he replied, a little lamely.

"Well, the hostilities must have been quite recent, then," said the lady with the green eyes. "You've got blood gushing down your leg like a waterfall. You'd better come home with me, young man, at once before you bleed to death."

Friday 29th April 2005

Hugo and Lisa strolled arm in arm together in Paris in the warm spring sunshine. They were halfway through their short break in the city and Hugo had booked a table for lunch at one of his favourite restaurants. It was quite early, however, and there was some time to kill. Arriving at Notre Dame, they decided against visiting the cathedral – far too many tourists – and proceeded instead eastwards and over the bridge to the Île Saint-Louis.

Lisa wanted to explore the boutiques along the trendy main street, the Rue Saint-Louis, but Hugo had other ideas. There was a little antiquarian bookshop he always liked to visit when he was in Paris, only a short walk away in the Latin Quarter.

"Do you mind if I go and visit my favourite bookshop whilst we're nearby?"

"Of course not."

"Why then don't we meet at the restaurant at, say, one fifteen… You know the way?"

"I'm sure I'll find it. See you there."

Hubert Lapiteau, a consummate bibliophile, had owned and run Hugo's favourite bookshop for many years. He recognised Hugo immediately as a regular customer, an Englishman who spoke French well. He had a good memory and a knack of sizing up his customers and of knowing just the sort of book that might interest them.

"I have just the book for you, Monsieur."

"You always do, Monsieur Lapiteau."

"Voila. It is a book of memoirs by Victor Chavigny. Chavigny lived here in Paris in the nineteenth century – a long and most interesting life. I have only had time to read a few chapters myself but enough to know that you will enjoy it, Monsieur… and for you I offer a special price of thirty euros."

Hugo took the book from Hubert and looked at it. It seemed

in quite good condition. 'Le Boulevardier Romantique' was the title. It was a weighty tome, though, and he feared it might be heavy going in more than one sense of the word. He said as much to Monsieur Lapiteau.

"Mais non, Monsieur. There is much to appeal in this book and it is a very rare one. Not many copies were printed originally, and a second edition was prevented by a libel action. I have not seen another copy for years. This may be the last available. I rob myself in letting you have it for such a price. Chavigny was a writer of erotic plays and verse, a typical Parisian boulevardier, a true flâneur, a great observer of life and above all…" and here Monsieur Lapiteau's voice dropped to a conspiratorial whisper "…a great seducer of women!"

Well, that settled it, of course.

"Oh, very well, Monsieur Lapiteau, I'll take it."

Hugo stepped outside and reached in his pocket for his mobile phone. He made a swift call to Gina in London to promise that he would come and see her just as soon as he returned home and to assure her that she was in his thoughts at every waking moment.

"Hugo, Frank's phoned me at least four times since you've been away. Do you think he's checking up on me? I mean, do you think he suspects something?"

"Of course not. He misses you, that's all, just like I do. Now stop worrying! I'll see you on Monday evening. And, Gina dear, do make sure you've got some of the Dom Pérignon in, there's a good girl."

Shaking his head, and wondering why Gina was going through this paranoid phase, Hugo took out his diary to look up another number. This time it was a local one. Finding it eventually, he made the call.

"Allo!" a female voice answered, almost at once.

It was Odette, whose surname Hugo had never taken the

trouble to learn and which probably changed from time to time in any event. He always called Odette when he came to Paris. He had first met her in a bar near Les Halles where she plied her trade as a common prostitute, but she had moved onwards and upwards since then to a chic apartment overlooking the Parc Monceau.

Yes, she could fit him in that afternoon; she could always fit Monsieur Hugo in, but only for a half-hour slot between a South American diplomat and a European Commissioner. Her fee for the full service was even more eye-watering than usual.

"C'est l'euro, mon cher!" she said apologetically.

Never mind. She was worth every dollar, pound, yen or euro. He would have no difficulty in making some excuse to Lisa. It would only be for half an hour, after all, and he would need a bit of exercise after lunch. Besides, Paris without Odette just wouldn't be Paris!

Happily, he tucked Victor Chavigny's memoirs under his arm and strolled back the short distance to the restaurant to meet Lisa.

He would have the Magret de Canard which they did so well, and order a bottle of the Château Montrose 1985 which he always enjoyed. He would have to drink most of it as Lisa didn't really like red wine. Not a prospect, one has to say, by which he felt in any sense daunted.

Vive la France, Vive Odette, Vive le dejeuner!

Wednesday 4th May 2005

In hindsight Hugo was not convinced that it had been entirely wise to let his flat in Earls Court when he moved in with Lisa. After all, he hardly needed the rent money now that Lisa was paying all the bills for everything. It might too have reduced the risk of his relationship with Gina being discovered if they had been able to use his flat as a discreet love nest instead of always using the company apartment where she lived – less chance of Frank suddenly bursting in on them.

Further, Lisa's father was not supposed to know that he and Lisa were actually living together. He was a little old-fashioned in matters of this sort, even though he and Lisa were properly engaged. This meant that when Frank came to town, Hugo had to move into a hotel or arrange to stay with friends.

Frank almost certainly did know, of course, in an unofficial sort of way, but Lisa was insistent in case her father was upset. It was all rather ridiculous, not to say inconvenient.

Nevertheless, there were compensations. The flat was let to two charming, if somewhat eccentric, ladies in their mid-fifties called Dulcie and Dora. Hugo had actually first met Dulcie some two years before when he had found himself sitting next to her at a lunchtime concert of Beethoven piano sonatas at St John's, Smith Square and he had struck up an unlikely friendship with her and her lifelong friend Dora. At about the time when his flat became vacant, it just so happened that she and Dora were looking for a new place to live as the lease on their previous abode was due to expire – a most fortuitous coincidence.

Neither Dulcie nor Dora had a regular job. Dulcie busied herself with charity work of one kind or another, while Dora attended to domestic matters. They enjoyed a modest private income derived mainly from Dulcie.

Dulcie Wakeham-Maltravers was descended from a large, quite grand family, whose former ancestral home, a late-seventeenth-century manor house somewhere in Leicestershire, merited an extensive mention in Pevsner and was now owned by the National Trust. Dulcie's ancestors included, over the centuries, generals, statesmen, and the odd bishop or two. Hugo, who was about as unabashed a snob as ever looked down a finely shaped nose, of course took great pleasure in boasting of his friendship with such a Grande Dame.

He was in the habit of collecting the rent personally on the first Wednesday of each month, and it was a day to which he greatly looked forward.

As usual, Dulcie opened the door of the flat and he stepped into the hallway. Above the hall table, Dulcie had hung a portrait of her late father. He was an ex-guards officer and country gentleman, and looked every inch the part. Dulcie was dressed just as her father was in the portrait: tweeds, shiny brown brogues and sporting a regimental tie. Dora appeared hovering in the hallway behind her, wearing a floaty, diaphanous pale pink garment liberally adorned with twinkling sequins, looking for all the world like a Christmas tree fairy brought to life.

Dulcie and Dora were very fond of Hugo. Indeed, Dulcie treated him in much the same manner as an old-fashioned grandmother might treat a wayward but favourite grandson. For his part, Hugo was equally fond of the two women and felt completely at ease in their company. His double life with Lisa and Gina, adoring fiancée and secret lover respectively, was a rewarding but exacting one. Events such as dinner with his friend Archie, lunches with chums, and the visits to Dulcie and Dora provided a valuable breathing space, a time of normality when he could be himself; a time, above all, when it was unnecessary to keep up pretences of any sort. They were equivalent to the intervals during the performance of an opera brimming with passionate music, complex twists and turns, loves and lusts, ruthless machinations and dramatic surprises.

"Hello, Hugo, my dear – punctual, as always! Shall we go to my room and transact our little business?"

"Yes, of course."

"Well, I'll go and get the tea ready then, shall I?" said Dora.

"Yes, dear. You do that… but don't put the kettle on just yet.

Hugo and I have a few things to talk about."

Dulcie closed the door of what had once been Hugo's own bedroom behind them. It was much as Hugo had left it except for more of Dulcie's family portraits hanging on the wall and the fact that the furniture had been rearranged slightly to accommodate a large Edwardian desk and a cane-seated chair.

The business to which Dulcie referred simply involved her fishing out from her desk and handing over a cheque for the month's rent which she had already neatly written out, dated and signed.

This little ceremony completed; Dulcie proceeded in a schoolmistress fashion to interrogate Hugo about his doings in the month since the previous rent day. Dora was never a party to these absorbing conversations. Presumably Dulcie judged that she would be far too shocked by what she heard or would simply fail to understand.

"Are you still seeing that woman?" Dulcie asked.

"What woman?"

"Oh, don't be obtuse, Hugo. The stepmother of your poor fiancée."

"Yes, of course."

"Disgraceful! When was the last time you saw her?"

"Yesterday."

"And what did you get up to?"

"Oh, you know, the usual bedroom antics…with champagne to follow, of course.

"Shocking! And were there other women, too?"

"Well, there was Odette in Paris," Hugo admitted.

"Paris? Odette?"

"Didn't I say? Lisa and I were in Paris last week and I renewed my acquaintance with Odette…"

Hugo proceeded to give Dulcie a slightly abridged account of his visit to Odette in her delightful apartment near the Parc Monceau, and how much it had cost him.

"Despicable! But how could you afford to pay this… harlot, who apparently charges so much for her services?"

"Lisa gave me some money. I told her I needed it to buy a birthday present for my mother."

"You lying hound! But what was poor Lisa doing while you were indulging yourself in this beastly fashion?"

"Oh, I sent her off to buy me a new tie at a little shop near the Place des Vosges. She's very good at choosing ties, and it always gives her great pleasure to buy things for me, you know."

"Good God! What a dreadful cad you are!"

Of course, Dulcie was not genuinely shocked by any of these revelations. On the contrary, she was totally enthralled. Hugo had to divulge a little more information, sometimes even embellishing his account, simply to satisfy Dulcie's appetite for salacious detail.

"Well, Hugo," she said, when he had quite completed the month's catalogue of infamy, "you should be absolutely ashamed of yourself. If my father was alive, he'd give you a jolly good horsewhipping!"

"I don't see why I should be so ashamed. I thoroughly enjoyed myself and so did everyone else!"

"Hugo, you're quite incorrigible!" Dulcie said, trying to look stern and disapproving, but incapable of stopping herself from emitting a low gurgling chuckle.

Hugo responded with a wide grin.

"Come on," she said, "we better go and join Dora for tea…"

"Yes, I suppose we'd better."

"And, Hugo…"

"Yes?"

"Hugo, you are a bad man, a very bad man, indeed!"

"I know," said Hugo, proudly.

In the flat's main room – a lounge-cum-diner – a magnificent tea had been laid out. The room, however, now possessed the aura of a quaint tea shop in a Cotswold village and the sight of it always brought a smile to Hugo's face.

The tea itself was a fine Orange Pekoe from the uplands of Kenya. Dora had no truck, of course, with ordinary tea bags. There was always a freshly baked cake of a traditional variety, and this month it was the turn of the Victoria sponge. In addition to the cake, there were potted shrimps, cress and cucumber sandwiches, as well as rum truffles, brandy snaps and chocolate éclairs. What a feast!

Hugo and Dulcie took their places at the table next to one another while Dora sat opposite and a fourth chair was occupied by Horatio, a large and rather fierce black and white cat, who stared around him in that haughty manner characteristic of the feline species.

"What about this opera, then, Hugo?" Dora said, opening the conversation.

"What opera?"

"Oh, you know. The opera found by that architect man in Bloomsbury. The one that some musical scholar – Wetherby, I think, is the name – says is by Mozart. There's been a lot about it in the press recently, and there's a programme on the radio this evening."

"Oh, that opera. Well, it's all a load of old rubbish, in my not so humble opinion. I don't believe Mozart ever actually wrote such an opera, though he may have intended to. Had he written it, it would surely have been performed, and we would know about it even if the score was subsequently lost. This man Wetherby has allowed himself to get carried away with his own enthusiasm."

"As a matter of fact," cut in Dulcie, "I happen to know Professor Wetherby. He's the patron of The National Society for Disabled

Musicians, one of the charities I do a bit of work for from time to time. He can be a bit pompous, but he's a nice enough old stick really…I tell you what, Hugo, I could get you an interview with him if you like. Music scholars may not exactly be the usual celebrity interview fodder, but with all the stuff about this opera at the moment, I think it might be of interest to a newspaper or magazine, don't you?"

"Do you know, Dulcie, I think that's a very good idea. I can think of one or two editors, off the top of my head, who'd leap at it. Could you really fix an interview?"

"Leave it to me."

"And what about you, Horatio? Do you think that this funny old opera is really by Mozart?" Dora asked Horatio, but Horatio continued to stare greedily at the potted shrimps and sensibly made no comment.

Finally, Hugo left to make his way back to the tube station. It had been a most enjoyable afternoon as usual and now he had the Wetherby interview to look forward to, always assuming that Dulcie was as good as her word. It would be quite a coup and do his reputation a power of good. It would be fun for once to be the envy of his rivals.

The two ladies watched him go through the window as he walked away up the street, turning to wave to them both before he finally disappeared from view.

"What a perfect gentleman!" Dora sighed, fondly.

"Hugo may be a gentleman in the sense of his class and upbringing, but in all other respects he's a complete bounder!"

"A bounder! What on earth do you mean, Dulcie? He's so… so charming. How could he be a bounder?"

"But he is one, I assure you."

"Well, when I was a girl in Harrogate I recall a young man came to tea with us, and do you know what, Dulcie?"

"No, dear, what?"

"He spread jam on the Yorkshire tea loaf. Mother said that only a complete bounder would do such a thing. I'm sure that Hugo would never do something like that. Butter yes, jam no!"

"I'm afraid, Dora, there are evils in this life even worse than spreading jam on one's Yorkshire tea loaf. In fact, come to think of it, I do believe that I spread jam on mine last time I stayed with my cousin in Whitby, but if your mother said it was wrong then I suppose it must be. Be that as it may, Hugo, I regret to say, has been guilty of far worse. He tells me about these things quite openly, you know. He thinks it amuses me – which I'm awfully ashamed to say it often does – but that doesn't, of course, excuse his shameful conduct."

"You don't mean things involving… women, do you, Dulcie?"

"Yes, I do. Furthermore, not only is Hugo a bounder, but considering the way he behaves, he is a cad, a rotter and a rogue, too!"

"Oh dear, oh dear," Dora said, beginning to sound quite crestfallen. "But, we're very fond of Hugo, aren't we, Dulcie?"

"Of course, we are. We love him deeply, and we so look forward to his visits," Dulcie replied, permitting herself a dreamy little smile.

Hugo didn't go straight home of course, but went to visit Gina at Beacon Court. She'd obviously been drinking and was in a rather prickly mood. He could always tell. No alluring smiles and the tone of her voice had changed gear from sexy to strident.

"Why are you so fucking late?" she demanded to know.

"Because today's the day I go to collect the rent from Dulcie and Dora. I've told you before…"

"How the fuck do you expect me to remember that?! C'mon then, we better go to bed or you'll be late for Lisa… not that I fucking care."

Even in bed the bickering continued.

"What on earth do you want to go and see those eccentric old women for anyway, for fuck's sake? Can't they send the cheque by post or pay the money through the bank or whatever?"

"Well, they give me tea… They may be a trifle eccentric, but they're very charming. In fact, their eccentricity is very much part of their charm."

"So, you prefer tea and biscuits with those women to me, do you?"

"Oh, it's not just biscuits, you know. I get the full works – cucumber sandwiches, Victoria sponge, rum truffles and—"

"Oh, for fuck's sake, Hugo!" she screamed and dug her long fingernails into his buttocks.

"Ouch, that bloody hurt, you stupid bitch."

With this, Gina dug the nails in again, even harder and longer this time, drawing blood. It took some while before he was able to pacify her, but Hugo had vast experience in dealing with tricky women and, in the end, he managed to calm her down and normal relations were resumed.

They parted company on quite good terms after a glass or two of champagne and Gina even apologised for her behaviour. This didn't do much, however, to compensate for the stinging pain in his bottom.

Later that day, as Hugo and Lisa prepared for the night, Lisa noticed something rather odd as Hugo was about to climb into bed.

"Hugo!" she exclaimed. "What on earth are those nasty marks on your bottom?"

"Oh… um… well, you see, I was scratched by an angry pussycat. I, um, trod on her tail. I mean, by mistake, of course."

Hugo felt rather pleased with himself to have come up with such a neat explanation and one which half reflected the truth in a metaphorical sort of way.

"But, but, Hugo, I can't quite understand how this cat…"

Quickly seizing the moment and the opportunity to fend off any more tiresome questions, Hugo quickly slipped into bed, took Lisa in his arms and got down to business, after which she fell almost instantly into a deep, contented slumber.

Hugo rolled over onto his side, and lying still, summed up the doings of the day as he often did in bed. It had been a rather busy one, he concluded: finishing an article for a magazine in the morning about the growing popularity of Vivaldi's operas; lunch at the club with a little too much claret than was good for him; the visit to Dulcie and Dora with all that entailed; the unfortunate episode with Gina, and finally, just when he needed to rest, he'd had no option but to extend himself, as it were, yet again. God, it all took some stamina! Suddenly Hugo felt very tired, and he too drifted quietly off to sleep, having quite forgotten, of course, to tune into Radio 4 to hear the programme about the Bloomsbury opera as he had promised himself he would.

♪

"For tonight's programme, 'Who wrote the Bloomsbury opera?', we are joined by leading musicologist Professor Justin Wetherby, music scholar, critic and writer Doctor Raymond Digby, Martin Holsworthy, the editor in chief of the magazine Opera House, and by the BBC's very own Rosalind Golding, whom regular listeners will, I'm sure, instantly recognise as the presenter of the weekly series 'Mozart and Friends' on Radio 3.

For the benefit of those of our listeners who may have missed the story so far, some six weeks ago the manuscript of an opera score was discovered in the course of refurbishment works to a property near the British Museum. With the score was a complete libretto in German based on the eighteenth-century Italian play The Servant of Two Masters by the Venetian playwright Carlo Goldoni. However, no reference to the composer of the work could be found in the manuscript, probably because a few pages of it, including the title page, are damaged or missing.

Professor Wetherby, who has carried out an initial review of the manuscript at the behest of the Royal Academy of Music, caused a great sensation in a recent radio interview when he expressed the view that the score may be that of a long-lost opera by Mozart – or at least a copy of it, as the manuscript found is not in Mozart's hand. I should add that Mozart did in fact write to his father Leopold indicating that he was writing a German opera based on Goldoni's play, and Professor Wetherby naturally cites this letter in support of his opinion.

Starting with you, Professor Wetherby, if I may, has anything further come to light over the last few weeks to cause you to alter your view?"

"No, not at all. A scientific study of the paper and ink used in the manuscript has been carried out and the results show that, whilst it is not possible to identify the source of the ink, the paper was manufactured in central Europe roughly between the years 1780 and 1800. Handwriting experts confirm that the libretto and the musical score are not in the same hand, but, based on the style of writing, believe that both writers came from somewhere in the same region."

"So, just to be sure of what you're saying – you maintain that the score found is a copy of an original score by Mozart which has been lost?" Doctor Digby asked.

"Yes, that is so."

"Surely the real point," Martin Holsworthy interjected, "is that there has been no known performance or publication of an opera by Mozart based on the Goldoni play, has there? Nothing more has been heard of it."

"Exactly!" said Doctor Digby with some vehemence. All the evidence surely indicates that Mozart abandoned the work, and that any music he had written for it he simply reused in another context? Indeed, there are a couple of concert arias which have been so attributed."

"Of course, I am well aware of the arias to which you refer," Professor Wetherby quickly responded, "and it may be that Mozart abandoned the opera to concentrate on other compositions, but then took it up again later."

"I must say," Rosalind Golding said, speaking calmly but forcefully, "that whatever the factual evidence may be, I, in common with Justin, have been struck by the sheer quality of the music. Some might find it difficult to imagine that any other composer would have been capable of writing music of such sublime beauty. That was your view, wasn't it, Justin?"

"Indeed, it was and still is!"

"Well, what about Haydn, for example?" There was an air of some impatience now in Doctor Digby's voice.

"What about him?" Justin Wetherby replied with a corresponding note of irritation.

"Well, I'm sure you'd concede that Haydn was a man of genius too, equally capable of producing the most sublime music."

"True, but so what?"

"Well, Haydn, of course, paid two visits to England in the last decade of the eighteenth century. The manuscript is not in Haydn's hand any more than it is in Mozart's, but it is not surely beyond the bounds of possibility that Haydn brought with him the score of a new opera which he had composed specially for the London stage and which was copied and edited for him for potential performance. The copy, which has now turned up, might, therefore, be a copy of an original Haydn opera. Haydn wrote several operas based on libretti by Goldoni and they were amongst his most successful. Why not repeat the winning formula?"

"But a German opera? All of Haydn's operas were in Italian."

"Not so. What about Philemon und Baucis?"

"Well, I meant, of course, Haydn's more significant operas. Philemon and Baucis was, after all, only a short opera for marionettes, was it not?"

"Still a German opera, though… Look, Justin, I'm not trying to say that the opera found in Bloomsbury was actually by Haydn, simply that this theory is at least as plausible as yours."

"You're forgetting the letter from Mozart to his father."

"That's so, and one might still think that nobody but Mozart could have composed this music!" Rosalind Golding repeated, striking a more emphatic tone.

"But, nevertheless, I find it amazing that an opera by Mozart of all people could have sunk without trace!" Martin Holsworthy reiterated, equally emphatically.

Miles Fenton, the presenter, fearing that the discussion was starting to get a little out of hand was about to say something but Justin Wetherby got in first: "Look. Perhaps Mozart concluded, as frankly I would, that The Servant of Two Masters would be better rendered as an Italian opera, but before an Italian libretto could be prepared, he ran out of time with the ever-pressing need to produce new compositions. Thus, his German opera was left in its then completed, or nearly completed state, but unperformed. Is that not a perfectly tenable explanation?"

Adam leaned over and turned off the old Roberts radio which lay on the bedside table on Sandra's side of the bed.

"Adam! I was, like, listening to that. It was very interesting."

"I know, but I feel like kissing you."

"Yes, but I wanted, like, to hear—"

But Adam stifled what Sandra had been about to say with a long, lingering kiss.

"Oh, Adam!" she gasped when their lips finally parted. "Oh, Adam!"

"Tell you what," Adam said, "if you give me the right answer to my next question, I'll take you to Chez Véronique. How about that?"

"You're horrid, you are! You're always asking me trick questions which you know I can't answer!" Sandra replied, hitting him over the head with her pillow.

"Well, this isn't a trick question, and I really hope you give me the right answer."

"Try me, then."

"Sandra, shall we get married?"

"Oh, Adam!" she said. "Oh yes, yes please!"

Friday 6th May 2005

Hugo had just started to read the morning paper, when the telephone rang. It was Dulcie.

"Hugo. Is that you? Look, I've managed to speak to old Wetherby. It took a bit of persuasion but he's agreed to give you an interview. All you have to do now is ring for an appointment."

"Dulcie, you're a gem. Thank you so much."

Dulcie gave him the number, and he promised to tell her all about it on the next rent day. As soon as she rang off, he telephoned the number she'd given him, which was answered promptly by an efficient-sounding female voice who announced herself to be Professor Wetherby's secretary. A date later in the month was fixed for Hugo to attend Wetherby's home in Wiltshire, somewhere not far from Salisbury.

It occurred to Hugo that he ought to conduct a little research into missing Mozart scores and so forth in preparation for the interview, but poring over dusty old papers and ancient tomes in library reading rooms was not quite Hugo's scene, if it could be avoided. Far better was to find some clever person who already knew the answers. By a happy coincidence he was due to have lunch at his club that very day with an old friend, Thomas Malinska. Thomas, the grandson of a Czech refugee, taught the violin and viola at the Guildhall School of Music and was an acknowledged scholar of late-eighteenth- and early-nineteenth-century music. No doubt he would have been closely following the Bloomsbury opera saga.

Indeed, the lunch turned out to be even more fruitful than Hugo had hoped. First, Thomas had filled Hugo in on the arguments surrounding the authenticity of the score as a potential Mozart discovery, which more than compensated for his missing the Radio 4 programme. But there was more to come.

"Tell me, Hugo. Have you ever heard of Magdalena Malinska?"

"No. Who is she, an aunt of yours or something?"

"Well, she was a famous ancestor of mine. Magdalena was born sometime in the middle of the eighteenth century, and was married to Josef Malinska, one of Prague's most prosperous merchants and an influential man of his time.

"Magdalena was reputed to be a great beauty, but was not perhaps the most loyal of wives. She had an affair with her daughter's music teacher, a rather dissolute young man, many years her junior, who fled to England just before Josef found out. It all caused a great scandal, of course."

"Really… but how is this relevant?"

"I'm coming to that. Family legend has it that Josef had found the manuscript of a previously unknown opera by Mozart at a lodging house he owned near the Charles Bridge, but that, on a whim, Magdalena gave it to this young man, her lover, as a parting gift. Neither he nor the opera, it seems, were ever seen or heard of again."

"Good Lord!"

"It's an interesting story, perhaps, but of course it doesn't really help with the question of the authenticity of the Bloomsbury score. Who could say that the opera score which Josef is alleged to have found was really by Mozart? And even if it was, there is no real evidence to connect this score with the one found in Bloomsbury other than the fact that Magdalena's lover apparently fled to England."

"Well, I confess that I have had my doubts, too, about this opera being a genuine Mozart discovery, but nevertheless this is a fascinating story, Thomas. It's wonderful, absolutely wonderful! The press will lap it up and it's just what I need to spice up the article I'll be writing following up my interview with old Wetherby… if you've no objection to my using it, that is?"

"No, of course not. But there's another matter of some interest, although you may not feel so inclined," Thomas added with a wry little smile "to include it in the piece on your Wetherby interview."

"What might that be?"

"Well, amongst the works comprised in the Malinska Collection of Fine Art, now on loan to the Sternberg Palace in Prague, there is a set of miniatures, all of them portraits, one of which depicts an unknown young man who is generally thought to be Magdalena's lover, the music teacher…"

"So?"

"Look, here's a picture of it."

Thomas produced a large tome entitled 'The Art of Bohemia' and turned to a page with a colour plate headed 'Set of nine miniatures forming part of the Malinska collection at the Sternberg Palace, Prague'.

"Now, Hugo… which one of those do you think is the music

teacher? His face will be familiar to you."

"How should I know?" Hugo responded, peering at them.

"Well, it's the one in the middle. Try looking in the mirror, Hugo, when you get home!"

Saturday 7th May 2005

Sandra sang the jaunty little aria 'Capricious Man' from Handel's oratorio Saul, and she sang it with gusto. She was enjoying herself now and her earlier feelings of nervousness had quite passed. The concert was nearly at an end, and she thought it had gone very well. All the soloists and the choir had sung their hearts out and she believed that she herself had never sung better. Of course, being ever self-critical, she thought she could have done even better still, but at the same time she was quietly confident that she'd done well enough to impress the famous Sir Marcus Lismore.

Foolishly, though, she had forgotten to ask Adam before the concert what Sir Marcus Lismore actually looked like. By the time the thought occurred to her it was too late. Adam was somewhere right at the back of the hall, helping to hand out the programmes. Surely, though, Sir Marcus would sit somewhere fairly near the front, wouldn't he? That should narrow the field.

Looking round the hall, there were a few giggly young girls who had taken the trouble to wear their party frocks and some of the middle-aged men were wearing their city suits. The rest of the audience were attired casually as if attending an impromptu barbeque party in their neighbour's back garden. It seemed to Sandra, whose views on such matters were surprisingly old-fashioned, a bit sad that people made such little effort to dress nicely for occasions like this. It was surely only polite when the singers and orchestra had expended so much time and effort in rehearsals. Too bad! This was the way things were today, and it wasn't as if St Vincent's Church Hall in Hammersmith was exactly St Martin-in-the-Fields. In any case, she had to admit that she was the last person to complain given that her very own dear Adam had turned up looking, as ever, as if he had spent the last two nights in a bail hostel.

The hall that evening was gratifyingly full and that's what really mattered after all. In fact, she told herself, the nondescript nature of the audience ought to make the job of spotting Sir Marcus that much easier. He wouldn't be one of the stripy suit lot, she thought, nor surely would he be wearing a pullover or a t-shirt or a tracksuit top. A man noted for his charisma and magnetic personality, he would stand out from the crowd, wouldn't he? One would notice him immediately.

Just before the concert was due to begin as the orchestra were tuning up, she saw a large, red-faced man making for a vacant seat in the middle of the second row. It was him, she was quite sure of it. He was wearing a fedora hat, silk scarf, red corduroy suit, and carrying a stick topped with a silver knob. A trifle flamboyant, perhaps, but if you're a 'Famous Man of the Arts', you are surely entitled to a little latitude in matters of dress, so Sandra reasoned. She resolved to maintain eye contact with him whenever she could.

A buffet supper had been arranged for the orchestra, choir and soloists after the concert, along with relations and friends. This was to be held in the crypt of the church itself next door to the parish hall where the concert took place, and Sandra made her way there as swiftly as possible as the food at these events, not to mention the drink, tended to disappear rather quickly.

She was tucking into a well-deserved sausage roll, washed down with a glass of red wine served from a cardboard carton, when she saw the large red-faced man in conversation with a member of the orchestra. Should she approach him, or wait for him to approach her? she wondered. The problem was resolved a moment or two later when Adam arrived with another man, an exquisitely dressed man with a head of flowing, well-groomed silver-grey hair. He looked every inch the great conductor.

"Hello, Sandra," Adam said, greeting her with a peck on the cheek. "This is Sir Marcus Lismore…" he continued. "Sir Marcus, may I introduce my fiancée, Sandra Grisewood."

How stupid! Sandra thought. How could I possibly have thought that ridiculous man in the second row could ever have been the great Sir Marcus Lismore?

"Oh, Sir Marcus," she said, after a slightly uncomfortable pause, as she struggled to come to terms with her mistake, "it was very kind of you to come to our concert. I hope you enjoyed it."

"I did indeed. Now, tell me, Sandra," he said, speaking in a cultured, beautifully modulated voice matching his elevated appearance, "do you find all men capricious? You seemed to take particular pleasure in that last Handel aria."

"Er, well, no… I mean only sometimes, some men…" Sandra replied, thrown off balance yet again.

"Not me, I hope!" Adam laughed.

Sir Marcus Lismore looked piercingly into Sandra's face. Many had wilted when faced with one of the 'Lismore Looks' and Sandra was no exception. There was about him an air of almost godlike authority.

"You have a beautiful voice, Sandra, and you sing with both intelligence and passion, though I suspect you have yet to reach your full potential. I believe I can help you… I would love to talk to you in more depth but now is not the time and I'm afraid I must be on my way. Here's my card. Please telephone my secretary to arrange an appointment. A bright future awaits you, Sandra, if you have confidence and dedication. You have much to offer."

With another of his piercing looks, accompanied by a polite nod towards Adam, the great man turned and walked away.

"Well, there you are then," Adam said when he had gone.

"Yes," Sandra replied, "there I am."

"You don't seem very excited about it, I must say. I'd be chuffed to bits if I were you. In fact, I'm quite chuffed myself even though I'm only me."

"Oh, I am excited, Adam, really I am… it's just that I'm a bit tired, and I can't quite take it all in."

But Sandra was not so much tired as pensive. Quite possibly this was a turning point in her life… but did she really want to turn? Her burning ambition, still red hot when the evening began, suddenly seemed to have fizzled out, leaving only flickering embers of uncertainty.

Did she really want to move on, as they probably would, from the snug little flat where she and Adam had been so happy?

Did she want to quit her job at the design studio where everyone had been so kind to her?

Would she not miss her evenings with the amateur operatic society which had been such fun and where she had made so many new friends?

Would she be prepared to sacrifice all these things on the altar of celebrity?

Did she, in fact, wish to exchange her cosy, happy little life for something entirely different; a small island for a large continent?

Of course, she knew she'd never forgive herself if she didn't grasp this opportunity, but… but…

Finally, did she really have the courage to make that appointment to see Sir Marcus Lismore again; a prospect which, it would be useless to deny, she found most horribly intimidating?

Oh dear! Oh dear!

Tuesday 10th May 2005

"Un espresso e un cannoncino alla crema, per piacere."

Dr Ernesto Tolentini placed his order as he stood at the bar at Tonolo in Venice. Tonolo was without question his favourite pasticceria, and the cannoncini, those little puff pastry cannons loaded with delicious creamy custard, were in his opinion quite the best to be found in the whole of the city. Happily, his wife Lucia forbore to criticise his waistline-expanding passion for cannoncini on the implicit understanding that he overlooked her wallet-evacuating obsession with handbags. Altogether they enjoyed the happiest of marriages based on a mutual tolerance of each other's little weaknesses.

The couple lived in a spacious and beautifully appointed apartment in the Campo Santa Margherita. It was very convenient for the Ca' Foscari, the University of Venice, where Ernesto lectured in Drama Studies. It was not far from Tonolo either, and dangerously close to a very good bag shop. Except for the occasional academic conference or lecture tour, he seldom travelled away from Venice or indeed on most days very far from the university itself, save for his daily visits to Tonolo. Why bother?

That morning Ernesto had reason to be pleased with himself.

First, he had finally managed to persuade his wife that it would not be a good idea for her widowed mother from Turin to come and live with them. He had put forward several good reasons, including the killer fact that the spare bedroom, being the only room available for her occupation, was crammed to capacity with a vast array of things accumulated over the long years of their marriage for which it would be impossible to find room elsewhere, not least a very large collection of handbags.

Secondly, he had at last finished the notes for a lecture which he was due shortly to deliver to a group of visiting academics from England under the title 'Bittersweet themes in European theatre'.

Ernesto spoke English well, but had had great difficulty in coming up with a good way to round off his talk. Suddenly, though, inspiration had come to him.

"Bittersweetness," he would say, "is the prevailing undercurrent of many of life's experiences, which is why it is such an important theme for writers and dramatists. Before you return to England, may I suggest you treat yourselves to some of our delicious Italian chocolate, both of the milk and dark variety. The milk chocolate is rich, creamy and sweet, while the dark chocolate is also rich in taste but with a slightly bitter flavour. So there you are, my friends: Italian chocolate – a metaphor for life!" His Italian colleagues would no doubt regard such a remark as silly and frivolous, but the English always appreciated a little joke. Excellent!

Finally, and by no means least, he had managed to locate some evidence which could have an important bearing on a current controversy, and which at the same time was sure to enhance his academic reputation. Naturally, as a leading Goldoni scholar, he had been following with great interest the unfolding story of the opera score and libretto found in London based on Goldoni's famous play The Servant of Two Masters. One of those proverbial little bells had tinkled in his mind. Noted for his prolific memory for a myriad of obscure facts, his mind resounded to the metaphorical sound of ringing bells quite as frequently as the real sound from any of the famous bell towers of Venice. It was, it must be said, a character trait which provoked as much irritation amongst his colleagues as it did astonishment.

Thirty years ago, at the time of researching his first book, entitled Carlo Goldoni and the Influence of the Commedia dell 'Arte on Eighteenth Century Comic Drama, he remembered coming across some correspondence, preserved at the Palazzo Centrani, which had been Goldoni's residence and was now the Museo Goldoni. The correspondence was exchanged between

Goldoni and the composer Baldassarre Galuppi, for whose operas Goldoni had provided several libretti during the course of a long collaboration. It had not seemed that significant at the time, but now in the light of the discovery of this manuscript it might, he thought, prove to be very important indeed. Ernesto recalled that the correspondence comprised just two letters: one from Goldoni to Galuppi and the other from Galuppi in reply. He recalled the gist of the exchange.

In the letter to Galuppi, Goldoni had suggested to the composer that his play The Servant of Two Masters might make a good plot for an opera and that he would be willing to prepare a libretto if Galuppi agreed. In Galuppi's reply to Goldoni, the composer had expressed his enthusiasm for the idea, and his view that the work would enjoy as much success as an opera as it had done as a stage play or words to that effect. Nothing further, however, was known about the matter. Possibly Goldoni's libretto, if he wrote one, had found its way to one of the German courts, Dresden perhaps, one of the larger and wealthier courts and one noted for the excellence of its musical traditions. Perhaps a German translation had been made there and it was a copy of this version which had eventually found its way to London. Ernesto was not himself an expert in music or opera, but if the libretto was indeed a German version of Carlo Goldoni's own, would it not also be logical to suppose, in the light of the correspondence, that the accompanying score might be that of his great friend, fellow Venetian and collaborator Baldassarre Galuppi? He would write that very afternoon to this English musicologist, Professor Wetherby, to expound his theory.

Ernesto consulted his watch. In ten minutes, his wife and daughter were due to meet him here at Tonolo. His daughter, a lecturer in medicine, was inclined to be censorious about his cannoncino habit. She would tick him off and lecture him severely about the perils of diabetes and other dreadful diseases that he would much rather not hear about. Still, there was just about enough time to have another one before they arrived. If he was quick, no one need know.

Thursday 12th May 2005

On a bright May morning, Katie sat at her desk on the first floor of the offices of Messrs Fletcher Pugh & Meadowfield, a firm of solicitors in a pleasant Shropshire market town. Katie was a trainee solicitor with the firm, the largest of the three legal practices in the High Street, with branch offices dotted around the local area.

One can only speculate as to how she came to be granted articles, or rather a training contract, as it is now more prosaically called, as she was by no means the best-qualified candidate, and had no particular connection with any partner or important client, past or present, but she had a nice figure, a pretty face and a most engaging smile, which must, one suspects, have played well for her at her interview.

Some weeks ago, Ted Meadowfield, one of the firm's older partners, had had the invidious task of conducting Katie's annual staff appraisal.

Ignoring most of the questions which occupied the body of the appraisal form, he had, much to the horror of the serious-minded young personnel partner, written in the space provided for additional comments:

"Without putting too fine a point on it, Katie is not the brightest young woman. Her grasp of basic legal principles is rudimentary at best, and, like so many of her generation, she appears barely able to express herself clearly and accurately in English. One wonders how she secured a place at university, let alone obtain a Law degree there, albeit a third-class one. On the other hand, Katie has the shapeliest thighs and a truly engaging smile. The mere sight of her is a tonic, particularly for a jaded old soul like me. Altogether, she is an adornment to the office, and one would like to believe that her future with the firm is assured."

That morning, Katie was busy looking through the contents of an old deed box which belonged to a Mrs. Foxley, an elderly client, who had passed away a few days before. Mr. Meadowfield had asked her to look through the box and dig out for him the deceased's last will, documents relating to her house and land and any other papers which might be relevant to the winding up of the estate, a task which he considered should not be beyond even her limited capabilities.

Katie had found the will, the property documents, a large gusseted envelope containing share certificates, and several old life insurance policies. She had also come across a fat leather-bound book with page after page of elegant, if spidery, writing in it. Anyone else would probably have concluded that this latter item was of little relevance to the estate, but Katie, being Katie, was unsure and added it to the pile of papers to take in for Mr Meadowfield to peruse. After combing her hair twice and applying a little more lip gloss, she gathered up all the documents and trotted along the corridor with them to old Mr. Meadowfield's office.

"I've got, like, the will, documents and stuff for Mrs.Foxy, Mr. Meadowfield."

"You mean Mrs. Foxley, Katie."

"Oh, yeah… sorry." Katie giggled. Such a delicious little giggle too, Ted Meadowfield thought. It was very difficult ever to be cross with her.

"You must try to remember, Katie, that in a lawyer's job, accuracy is everything," he said patiently.

"I'll try very hard next time, Mr. Meadowfield. Promise."

"Well, if you'd just put everything on my desk here," he said, indicating a part of the desk which was relatively free of other papers, "I'll have a look at it all in just a moment."

Katie plonked the documents down as she was bidden, taking care to lean over the desk so that Mr. Meadowfield would get a better view of her cleavage, of which she was most justifiably proud.

"Will that be all, like, Mr. Meadowfield?" she said, flashing him one of her most engaging smiles and giving a little wiggle of the shapely thighs

"Yes, yes, Katie. Thank you." In truth it was more than enough for poor old Ted, who feared that his blood pressure might have just taken a sudden upward leap.

As Katie turned and left the room, Ted addressed himself, with a deep sigh, to the pile of documents. The will was quite straightforward. As Mrs. Foxley's husband had predeceased her, her estate and effects were to be equally divided between her three adult children after payment of inheritance tax and some legacies in favour of the local church and a donkey sanctuary in South Devon. He and his partner Graham Pugh were appointed as executors.

The property where Mrs Foxley had resided, an impressive black and white timber-framed farmhouse dating from the Elizabethan period, formed part of the Foxley Manor estate and had belonged to the Foxley family for many generations, though the manor itself had been sold off and most of the land still belonging to the farm was tenanted by local farmers. As the Foxley title went back over many centuries there was a goodly pile of old deeds and documents, along with the current tenancy agreements. Though the title was now registered at the Land Registry, Ted was, however, unable to resist a look at the old historical deeds and enjoyed the thought that some lawyer centuries ago had pored over them, just as he was doing now. He even enjoyed the waxy feel of the old deeds themselves; not perhaps quite in the same league, as sensations go, as embracing young Katie under the mistletoe at the firm's Christmas party and the feel of her soft lips against his old cheek… but there it was. Next Christmas seemed a long way off.

Oh dear! When one reached a certain time of life, Ted thought sadly, one simply had to make do with lesser pleasures. Mind you, he had looked at himself in the bedroom mirror that morning and on the whole, he didn't seem too bad for his age – a full head of hair, even if it had now turned grey, tall with an upright posture and, he thought without undue modesty, a quite distinguished appearance. A bit of a gut, he had to admit, but a man must surely be allowed a little leeway after a lifetime of work in the law, whatever his wife Marjorie might say. Katie always seemed quite flirtatious. Was this just her nature, or was she trying to tell him something? Vain hope! he told himself, you silly old fool… but on the other hand, one never really knew where women were concerned, did one?

Just as he had made a start on the rest of the papers which Katie had brought in, he noticed amongst them the leather-bound volume which she had also found in the deed box. It seemed to be the journal or diary of one Eleanor Foxley, who was married to Sir Charles Wilberforce Foxley, the sixth baronet, of whom Mrs Foxley's late husband was an indirect descendant. Presumably the diary had passed down through the generations. Since, though, it had been put away with the deeds, nobody would probably have looked at it for years.

Later research would show that Eleanor was born in the year 1760 into a prosperous local family, whose wealth was based on the wool trade. Anxious to ascend the social scale, her father had acquired a substantial house whose land adjoined that of the Foxley Manor estate.

The couple had met at the Twelfth Night Ball held annually at Foxley Manor. Eleanor had greatly enhanced her social standing by marrying Sir Charles, who had in turn benefited financially from the match; a classic union of cash and acres.

Ted turned to the first entry in the diary which was dated the 25th April 1782. The writing was not too difficult to decipher. It read:

Today, we began our great adventure. It was a wonderful spring morning and the sun flooded the courtyard where our carriage stood ready to depart. The old manor, our home, had never appeared to me more lovely. The honeyed hue of its stone façade enhanced by the bright sunshine seemed truly to cast a warm glow upon us as if begging us not to venture forth but to stay forever wrapped in its friendly embrace. Why after all should we ever think of leaving such a beautiful place?

Presently, though, the carriage moved off. The servants lined the driveway to see us on our way. My Caro Sposo sat grim-faced. Words were lost to him. I do believe he felt the pang of departure even more keenly than I. It was all I could do to persuade him to smile and raise his hand to acknowledge the servants' farewell to us. Two of the housemaids were in tears I could not help but observe.

Soon we were past the gatehouse and after a few miles the familiar farmhouses, woods and fields belonging to the estate were no longer to be seen. The spire of our village church was the last of the fondly remembered landmarks to disappear from view.

Poor Charles uttered a deep long sigh. I tried to cheer him with thoughts of the sights we were to see during the forthcoming months of our travels. I talked of the beautiful city of Paris, the great lake of Geneva, the majestic mountains of the Alps, of Turin, of Mantua, of the canals, churches and palaces of Venice, of the jewel-like duomo of Florence, the Uffizi, the Baptistery, the Ponte Vecchio, of the glories of the eternal city of Rome, the grand city of Naples, and finally Sicily

This evening we reached Wycherley Court where we stay as guests of Lord and Lady Leffingham for two nights. My dearest love remained in a sullen mood and his spirits only lifted after dinner as the ladies left the table to allow the gentlemen to enjoy their own company with the port wine. It will be some days before we reach the coast and take ship for France. I shall not feel our journey has truly begun until we reach foreign soil.

So, the couple had set off to make the Grand Tour, as so many did in those days. 'Most interesting,' Ted thought, 'most interesting.'

It so happened fortuitously that he was due that day to have lunch with the curator of the town museum, an old friend of his, and he thought that he might show him the diary for his opinion. He doubted that it would be of any great monetary value, but it might well be of historical importance.

Lunch was fixed for one o'clock at Forbes, a restaurant near the firm's offices, noted for its good food. A talented chef from London had taken the place over a year or so ago, and his signature dish, whole roast water vole cooked in its own jus with juniper berries and wrapped in a pastry parcel, had earned many accolades in guide books and foodie magazines. The menu dégustation was not for the thin-walleted, and it was unfortunately Ted's turn to pay – a trifle unfair since lunch the previous month had consisted of steak pie and chips at the King's Head. Well, his friend would have to do something in return now to earn his lunch.

The curator had a good look at the diary over the coffee and petits fours and advised that it might indeed turn out to be of some importance. He kindly offered to refer it to a cousin of his who happened to be a social historian at Manchester University by the name of Professor Edwin Bleddoes. The beneficiaries, who had hitherto been unaware of the existence of the diary, were in full agreement with this course of action, and so the matter was arranged.

Professor Bleddoes was most enthusiastic. On an initial cursory examination, the diary indeed promised to be of much interest. Essentially, as Ted surmised, it chronicled a 'Grand Tour' of Europe upon which Eleanor had embarked with her husband a year or so after their marriage, passing through France and the famous cities of northern and central Italy, before Naples and finally Sicily. The return journey, as the diary would reveal, had taken a different route through parts of central Europe and the Low Countries. Altogether the couple were away for nearly two years.

In fact, Eleanor's diary would come to be regarded as a significant and authoritative historical source because of the wealth of detail it contained, not least the description of an episode which would turn out to have an important bearing upon a certain contemporary musical controversy.

Of course, the local paper, the *Morning Post,* eventually got hold of the story of the diary's discovery. Foxley was a well-known local name. Foxley Manor itself, still so called, was now an expensive private nursing home. A statue of General Sir George Foxley stood proudly outside the council offices, there was a Foxley Memorial Theatre, Foxley Church of England Primary School, Foxley Health Centre in Foxley Manor Road, and until his death the late Mrs Foxley's husband had been the local

Member of Parliament. The Post wanted a photograph and by a happy coincidence Professor Bleddoes was due to visit his cousin, the museum curator, and agreed to bring the diary back with him so it might be displayed.

So it was that outside the offices of Messrs Fletcher Pugh and Meadowfield there stood, lined up for the *Post's* photographer, Ted Meadowfield, William Foxley, Mrs Foxley's eldest son, Professor Bleddoes holding aloft the diary itself and, of course, Katie, who had found the diary in the first place. Katie was undoubtedly the star of the occasion. She was dressed for the camera in a most revealing outfit which left little to the imagination and pretty much everything to the prurient fantasies of the *Post's* readership. The thighs had never seemed shapelier, the cleavage deeper or the smile more engaging.

The family basked in reflected glory and the firm basked in the welcome publicity, both equally delighted. Additionally, Ted's partners agreed that he should be reimbursed the cost of his rather expensive lunch with the curator of the town museum. Seldom had a circle been more agreeably squared.

Ted conceived of the wonderful idea of taking Katie out for a meal after the photographic session as 'a reward for finding the diary'. She had readily agreed and he said he would walk home to fetch his car and pick her up outside the bank in Shrewsbury Street in twenty minutes. This was a convenient way to arrange matters as it would not, he thought, be a good thing to be seen leaving the office with her. He had no wish to set tongues a-wagging. For much the same reason, he had decided not to take her to Forbes Restaurant nearby, where there were sure to be one or two of his partners lunching with clients, but instead to a country restaurant called The Holly Bush in a charming village setting about seven miles distant.

Katie, who was not in fact quite as silly as Ted imagined, was very pleased. She liked Ted Meadowfield. In fact, she liked older men generally – rich older men anyway.

Young men had their uses of course, but rarely had they any style these days. They just didn't know how to treat a girl properly or didn't care. Terry, her current boyfriend, if you could call him that, who worked for a local firm of estate agents, was a case in point. The last time she had been out with him, he had taken her to the Cricketers Arms, a busy pub on the Ludlow Road. He had spent virtually the entire evening talking to his mates while completely ignoring her, except for asking her what she wanted to drink. At closing time, it had been off to the Moti Mahal in the town centre for a swift chicken jalfrezi, and then back to his miserable little flat in the modern block behind Tesco so he could have his way with her. Terry was a tall young man with a handsome tanned face and a certain laddish charm. He certainly set the heart of many a young office girl all a flutter, but Katie had become rather bored with him, comparing him unfavourably with other older men of her acquaintance.

First, she contrasted him with Dennis, the fifty-eight-year-old marketing director of a large retail clothing business. Dennis had taken her with him to Milan for a trade fair and fashion show. They had spent a champagne- and Viagra-fuelled weekend in the sumptuous gilded luxury of a very grand hotel near the Piazza del Duomo, which once had been a Renaissance palace. Naturally, Dennis drove a big fat expensive motor car, took her to posh oak-panelled restaurants and regularly presented her with enormous bouquets of flowers and other pricey tokens of his affection.

Then there was the dear old retired Colonel who owned the big white house on the edge of town. He took her for long drives in the country in his lovely old Bentley convertible with whitewall tyres and had bought her a beautiful pearl necklace with matching earrings. Occasionally she caught him taking a sly little peep down her cleavage. He often patted her bottom, too, in an avuncular sort of way and sometimes his hand was apt to linger there a little longer than might strictly be regarded as proper, but otherwise all he ever wanted in return for his many kindnesses was the pleasure of enjoying, however briefly, the company of a pretty young woman. A real gent the Colonel was!

And now she had her boss, old Ted Meadowfield, nicely coming to the boil. He was a real gent too and such a sweetie. Soon his sleek silver-grey Jaguar rounded the corner and stopped outside the bank to pick her up as arranged.

"Mr Meadowfield," she said, after they had gone a little way.

"Yes, Katie?"

"I hope you don't mind me asking, but is that, like, a new suit you're wearing today?"

"Yes, as a matter of fact it is. I had it made for me by my tailor in London. I collected it only last week after that conference with Counsel at Lincoln's Inn I had to attend."

"I think you look very smart in it. Everyone was, like, saying so in the office this morning, even that old cow Maureen in Accounts."

"Well thank you, Katie."

"Of course, you're a very handsome man and you'd look smart in anything you wore…"

"You flatter me, Katie."

"You know, Mr Meadowfield," Katie continued, "I don't want, like, to embarrass you or anything, but I do really prefer older men… mature men like you, Mr Meadowfield, if you know, like, what I mean."

The world swam before Ted's eyes and everything went quite blurred for a moment or two. He shot a red traffic light and a white van swerved to avoid him with much hooting and rude gesturing.

Soon, thankfully, they were out of the busy market town and

motoring in open countryside through gently undulating hills. Ted felt a soft, podgy little hand gently descend upon his knee. For an instant he again lost control of the car, which lurched drunkenly across the carriageway, only just missing a collision with an oncoming Range Rover towing a horse box.

After the short, if perilous, journey to The Holly Bush, Ted, with some relief, pulled off the road into the car park reserved for patrons. Katie wiggled her way out of the car, smiled most engagingly and took Ted by the arm. Thus, they made their way together up the short gravel path towards the welcoming doorway. A shapely thigh brushed against him as they walked. This was pure magic, Ted thought, barely able to contain himself. He felt twenty years younger already!

As they entered the restaurant, they were confronted, much to Ted's surprise, by a large gathering of twittering middle-aged ladies in the cosy little bar, all members of the local Ladies Book Club assembled for their annual luncheon party. In their midst, sipping a very dry sherry by the inglenook fireplace, stood the steely-eyed figure of their current chairwoman, Mrs Marjorie Meadowfield, Ted's own beloved spouse.

Friday 20th May 2005

"Mother, you remember Mrs Belcanto, Lisa's stepmother. You met her at our engagement party."

"Of course, I do. It's very nice to see you again, Mrs Belcanto… but where's Lisa?"

"Oh, Lisa has gone away for the weekend to stay with her father up north. Gina thought she'd take a day off from work for a drive in the country, so we're going for a little tour in the luxurious company Mercedes around some pretty villages and having lunch at a place in Woodstock."

"I see. So, you won't be staying for lunch here?"

"No, not today. Just a flying visit, I'm afraid."

"Well, why not pop in for tea on your way back to London?"

"I'm afraid I don't think there'll be time, Mother. Got to get back to town quite early, you know."

"Ah, well, let me offer you some coffee, at least."

After coffee and biscuits, Gina asked if she might use the facilities.

"First right, past the grandfather clock in the hall, my dear."

When Gina was safely out of earshot, Mrs Belcher turned to her son.

"You're having an affair with that woman, aren't you, Hugo? I could tell by the way you look at her… and now this jaunt with her in the country."

"Mother, really! What are you saying?!"

"It's no use lying to me, Hugo, I know you too well. You always were a rotter so far as women were concerned. It's quite obvious to me that you're only marrying that poor little drip of a girl for her money. I know, I married your father for much the same reason, only to find that the little so-and-so wasn't anything like as rich as he made himself out to be. Of course, I realise Lisa's hardly likely to satisfy your beastly desires and you want something on the side. Well, all I can say is that it would be better to choose someone other than your prospective father-in-law's wife. She's a tart anyway!"

"Mother!"

"Oh, don't pretend to be so shocked, Hugo. I know Gina looks very sophisticated, well-dressed, superbly coiffed and all that, but at bottom she's just a tart. Lovely figure, very glamorous, but…"

"Sssh, Mother, she's coming back."

"My mother knows about us," Hugo said to Gina as she reversed the car out of his mother's driveway.

"You didn't tell her, surely?"

"No… she just knows. I could never keep any secrets from her. We're very alike my mother and I, that's the trouble. I knew it would be a mistake to come here."

"Well, I wanted to see where she lived. You're always telling me what a picturesque place it is. She won't say anything, will she?"

"No, of course not. She understands. She thinks you're fantastic. Very broad-minded, my mother."

"Good for her!"

In fact, Hugo and Gina were not returning to London until the following day. Taking advantage of Lisa's absence, they had booked into a romantic little hideaway for the night.

Later, they arrived, accordingly, at the Pemberton Arms and checked in. Since the war the place had changed hands several times but had always remained a rather ordinary roadhouse until recently when it had been taken over yet again and turned into a trendy gastro pub with rooms. The nasty modern additions which had been made to it over the years had been removed and it had been restored very tastefully. In many ways, it now looked more like the charming old coaching inn that it originally was than it had looked for many a year, though of course it was now a good deal smarter. One reviewer had, with conscious or unconscious irony, described it as a 'designer coaching inn'. As an added bonus, there was a fine view to the rear of Pemberton Hall, a grand country house built in the Palladian style, now a conference centre.

As they sat in the comfortable bar sipping their pre-dinner dry Martini cocktails, Hugo's eye was drawn to a portrait above the mantelpiece. It was an early-nineteenth-century painting in the naive mode depicting a meet of the local hunt in front of the inn. Standing in the doorway was a large, jolly man with a bulbous red nose, presumably the landlord, one arm raised to wave the huntsmen off and the other around the waist of a smiling, rosy-cheeked young woman exceptionally well-endowed in the bosom department.

Well, well, well! You lucky old fellow! Hugo thought, addressing himself to the painting.

He turned to face Gina again. She had finished her dry Martini, and was in animated conversation with a handsome young French waiter, who had come to take their order. His mother was right, he had to admit. She was a tart – a pretty posh one it was true, but a tart all the same. Not that he was complaining. He had always found tarts so much easier to rub along with, and he wasn't about to give up Gina whatever his mother might say. Curse her!

Sunday 2nd December 1804

Napoleon Bonaparte took the crown of gilded laurel leaves, placed it on his head and declared himself to be Emperor of France.

On the same chilly day in December 1804 as this extraordinary act of hubris took place in the great cathedral of Notre Dame, another event was about to unfold, not far away, at an old merchant's house on the Île Saint-Louis, an event no less momentous for the parties involved.

The old merchant himself, at least, that is to say, the last in a long line of old merchants to have owned and occupied the house, had been dead for some years, but his much younger widow, Madeleine Lagrange, was very much alive. She had inherited, on his death, the house, a matchless collection of ornate sword sticks, which had been old Monsieur Lagrange's pride and joy, and, happily, a very substantial personal fortune.

A rare red-headed beauty, Madeleine possessed the most bewitching pair of green eyes by which any man, upon whom her gaze luckily happened to fall, would surely be completely entranced. It was these beautiful eyes into which Antoine had found himself staring some six months before in the Church of St Louis, the blood dripping from his left buttock.

She stood very erect and somewhat formidable, looking down upon Antoine, who in turn looked up at her, crouched upon one knee. He had adopted this somewhat unnatural, not to say uncomfortable posture, believing it to be appropriate in the light of what he was about to say.

"My dearest Madeleine, would you do me the great honour of consenting to become my wife?" he said, feeling most frightfully self- conscious. He had made all sorts of proposals to women during his life, most not involving any honour at all – indeed almost all of them of an entirely dishonourable nature – and all these proposals he had managed to make without the slightest difficulty or embarrassment. Why was it, then, that when he was actually trying to do the honourable thing for once, he felt so damnably embarrassed? It was all very mystifying.

One might imagine that having a pistol ball dug out of one's left buttock would not be the most promising start to a romance, but within the week Antoine and Madeleine had become lovers, and he had remained with her at the house on the Île Saint-Louis ever since she had brought him home from the church on the fateful day of the shooting. For one thing, he could not very well have returned to his lodgings, where Maître Pincheau would know where to find him. For another, he had no money and little prospect of immediate employment to replace his appointments at the Pincheau and Duboisset households. Doors of other households, where he had had existing teaching engagements, were barred to him when news of the Pincheau affair became known, as they had been in England in similar circumstances.

Those of a cynical caste of mind might say that marriage to Madeleine, the wealthy widow, was simply a convenient way for Antoine to resolve his difficulties, and of course it was, but this would not have been fair either to Antoine or indeed to Madeleine, an intelligent and sensible woman, who understood a thing or two about men.

The fact was that Antoine was not simply Madeleine's lover in the way that he had been a lover of many women. He was genuinely in love with her – real love. Hitherto, he had always believed that love was an illusion by which poor romantic fools allowed themselves to be deluded, but now he had discovered that it was he who had been the fool all along. It had taken him some time to reach this conclusion, but it had dawned on him finally when he realised that life without Madeleine would be quite simply unbearable, even for a single day… Thus it was that he came to be kneeling awkwardly before her, looking up into her face with an expression of dog-like devotion, at almost the very same moment when 'that Corsican upstart Bonaparte', as Madeleine dismissively referred to him, was nearby busy cementing his imperial authority.

"Yes, of course I will," Madeleine replied, after a suitable pause, accepting Antoine's proposal. "Now, for God's sake get up off the floor. You look ridiculous down there."

Antoine gratefully struggled to his feet.

"Now, there are two conditions," Madeleine continued.

"I will agree to anything."

"You haven't heard what they are yet."

"Well, what are they, then, my fondest love?"

"First, you must never lie to me. You see, I know that you will have liaisons with other women…"

"No, no!" Antoine protested.

"Do you mean to say that you don't accept my condition?"

"Yes, of course I do. I mean that I won't be having any liaisons – not anymore."

"There, you see you are lying to me already!"

"No, no!"

"There you go again. But let me explain, when I say I don't want you to lie, I don't mean you should burden me with the whole truth."

"But if I am not to lie and I am not to tell the truth, what am I to say? What, pray, do you mean?"

"Oh, don't be so obtuse, Antoine. It doesn't become you. I simply mean that I want you to be discreet."

"Well, I'm always discreet, but…"

"Very well then. You have clearly accepted my first condition. Let there be no more ifs and buts about it."

"Well, if you say so. Now, what is this second condition of yours?"

"The second condition is that you should forthwith rid yourself of that dreadful waistcoat – the one you persist in wearing almost every day. The one indeed you are wearing now."

"But it is my favourite. I bought it in London. It is of the very best silk, beautifully embroidered and it cost a king's ransom."

"I dare say, but it looks worn and scruffy now. Besides, I don't like to think of all those other women in whose presence you must have worn it, or rather in whose bedrooms you must have removed it. No, I insist that it be thrown in the Seine this very instant. I will gladly pay for a new one."

"Oh, very well."

"Good. All that's settled then. Now, I would suggest the church of St Louis as a suitable place for the celebration of our wedding, if you have no objection. We met there, and it was there, indeed, that I married Monsieur Lagrange. He was a good man, and I'm not sure that he would entirely have approved of you, but there it is. You may now kiss me."

Antoine folded her in his arms and kissed her fondly.

"My dear sweet Madeleine," he said. "I love and adore you more than I can possibly say."

Antoine had spoken these words before, of course, or words very like them, on countless occasions in towns and villages, grand houses and country inns, in and out of bed, in bright sunshine and under the stars of the night sky, but this was the first occasion on which he had truly meant them.

It was a shame about the waistcoat, though.

Tuesday 24th May 2005

Luxbrough House, a jewel of a small country mansion built in the reign of William and Mary, lies in its own secluded grounds on the edge of a pretty Wiltshire village of flint cottages a few miles to the north of Salisbury. It had been the home of the Wetherby family since about 1721 when it was acquired from its original owners who had lost a great fortune, caught unawares by the bursting of the South Sea bubble in 1720, as people so often are by bursting bubbles.

Professor Justin Wetherby himself now stood by the window of his study on the first floor on a bright morning in late May, looking out over the little trout stream which passed through the grounds.

The weather was quite warm, and there had been a hatch of mayflies. He could just see them fluttering and bobbing in their nuptial dance over the surface of the water. The ranunculus weed waved its thick green fronds rhythmically with the flow of the stream. An occasional trout rose to snatch a mayfly that had fallen back on the surface. A kingfisher flashed by upstream. Old Harry, the gardener, pottered to and fro, tending the rose bushes and herbaceous borders. The bees buzzed, the birds tweeted, and all was well with the world, but not with poor Professor Wetherby. The idyllic serenity of the scene was entirely lost on him. He was in a fretful frame of mind, for which a combination of factors was responsible.

He had of course expected his views on the Bloomsbury score to be controversial, but he had not frankly anticipated the venomous reaction of some of his fellow academics, one of whom had even publicly referred to him as "a silly, misguided old fool", nor had he bargained with the degree of media intrusion which he was beginning to find extremely irksome.

Then there was this letter he had recently received from some fellow by the name of Ernesto Tolentini, a lecturer in drama at Venice. It was couched in polite, slightly old-fashioned English prose, full of overblown, sometimes rather mystifying phrases slightly reminiscent in style of the brochure for the charming hotel in Positano where he and his wife had once spent an Easter holiday. On the evidence of some correspondence unearthed by this worthy individual, Goldoni may possibly have prepared a libretto based upon his play The Servant of Two Masters to be set to music by his compatriot, the composer Baldassarre Galuppi, with whom, as is well-known, he had collaborated in the preparation of several operas. Was it not possible, the letter contended, that the score found in London was of a German version of a missing opera by Galuppi based on a translation of Goldoni's own libretto?

In signing off the letter, Tolentini had even had a stab at a bit of humour, claiming himself to be 'the servant of two masters' – the muse of Goldoni and the music of Galuppi. From the tone of his letter, this Italian chap was evidently a charming fellow, but Wetherby could frankly have done without his intervention at this stage. Tolentini might be a Goldoni scholar but he was not a musicologist. He hadn't seen the score and wouldn't have had a clue about its provenance even if he had.

Clearly, in Wetherby's view, the music of the Bloomsbury opera was in a later style than any of Galuppi's operas. However, in the light of the acknowledged connection between Goldoni and Galuppi the theory was not one which could simply be dismissed out of hand.

Next there was Raymond Digby's idea on the radio programme that the opera might have been composed by Joseph Haydn. Digby was a man with whom Wetherby had frequently found himself at academic loggerheads and who happened, Wetherby knew, to be a close personal friend of the man who had called him a silly old fool. Haydn was a great composer, as Wetherby would have been the first to acknowledge, but enchanting and under-valued as his operas might be they did not really represent the summit of Haydn's oeuvre. If the score had been that of a symphony, a string quartet or a setting of the Mass, Haydn would indeed have been a strong contender, but not, in Wetherby's opinion, in the case of this opera. Nevertheless, the Haydn theory was not one either which could easily be rejected.

One might have thought that Professor Wetherby, as a dedicated professional musicologist, would have welcomed the opportunity to explore alternative theories, but he simply found them a nuisance. He was completely convinced, partly by the undisputed fact that Mozart had at least started to write such an opera and partly by the superb quality of the music itself, that the opera was indeed a lost Mozart masterpiece. It had become his sacred mission to prove it.

The final and more immediate cause of his fretfulness, however, was that in a weak moment and at the urging of that woman Dulcie Maltravers, he had agreed to be interviewed by some journalist. This wretched man, Hugo somebody or other, was due to arrive at any moment and the truth was that he simply didn't feel up to it that morning, not at all.

Just then his wife Alice entered the room with a cup of tea. They were a devoted couple, having first met each other as students at university many years ago where Justin was an organ scholar and Alice a cellist.

"What's the matter, dear?" She asked on entering the room. "You don't look yourself."

"No… things have been getting me down a bit lately, but the main thing is that I've got this man, this journalist fellow, coming to see me this morning, and well… er…"

"You'd rather not see him, is that it?"

"Yes, I really don't want to see him. I don't feel up to it today, not at all, and I'm very busy too, what with the conference in Vienna coming up soon. I should never have agreed to the interview in the first place."

"Now, don't you worry, my dear. I'll simply send him away."

"Send him away? But, but how?"

"I shall tell him you had to go to London to meet Professor Goldenkopf from Heidelberg."

"But that's tomorrow."

"Yes, but he won't know that, will he? It's as near the truth as matters. After all, what's in a day?"

Entirely defeated by this wonderful example of female logic, Justin Wetherby happily capitulated. A mood of spring-like optimism, reflecting the sunny weather outside in the garden, asserted itself, and the dark brooding cloud hanging over him swiftly dispersed.

A bell sounded in the hall below.

"That'll be him, now," said Alice. "I'd better go down."

Hugo had driven down to Luxbrough House in Lisa's new little red sports car. He drove it much more frequently than Lisa these days, and indeed had appropriated it more or less entirely for his own use. So much more fun than the dreary old banger he used to drive.

It was a lovely day as he bowled along towards Salisbury with the top down. There was not a cloud in the sky, which seemed to him a perfect metaphor for life in general. His life anyway, which, after all, when all was said and done and being brutally honest about it, was all that really mattered to him.

He found the village without difficulty and on enquiry at the local pub was told that Luxbrough House was to be found only about half a mile or so further on beyond the church at the end of the village street. Soon, he found himself proceeding up the curved driveway. "What a house!" he said out loud to himself as he caught sight of it for the first time through the trees.

Perhaps he could persuade Lisa or her father to buy a place in the country. That would be a good idea. Lisa wanted to keep her job in town after they were married, but there would be nothing to prevent Hugo from travelling down early for the weekend… with Gina perhaps. It would have to be a house of some pedigree, of course, with statues, fountains, walled gardens and things; a house like this one, in fact. Perhaps Wetherby would take an offer, he thought rather mischievously. That would be nice. He must be getting on a bit, after all. High time, surely, for the old boy to move off to some seaside retirement home in Sidmouth or somewhere.

Still, these were thoughts for the future. Now was the time to concentrate on the business for which he had come here: the interview, by which he hoped to steal a march on his professional peers. After parking the car to one side of the driveway in the front of the house, he crunched his way over the gravel to the front door and rang the doorbell.

Alice Wetherby opened the door to him. She was quite tall, and despite her age, was blessed with strong, fine features. She must, Hugo thought, have been a very beautiful woman when she was younger.

"Good morning, my name's Hugo Belcher, and I've an appointment with Professor Wetherby at eleven."

"I'm sorry, Mr Belcher, but my husband's not at home. He had to go to London to meet a visiting professor of music from Heidelberg."

"But, but… I've just come all the way from London to see him down here."

"Yes, well, I'm afraid there was some confusion over the dates, and…"

"Confusion?! The appointment was made over two weeks ago, and it was confirmed in writing!"

"Well, you could hardly expect my husband to alter an important engagement for a mere journalist, could you?!"

With this splendid retort, Alice firmly banged the front door shut, leaving Hugo standing spluttering in the porch. A little guiltily, she stepped into the dining room, which overlooked the forecourt and drive. Peeping discreetly through the window, she watched Hugo, with a face like someone intent on mass murder, walk back to his car. Within seconds he was driving away very fast up the driveway, wheels spinning, scattering gravel into the rose beds, weaving from side to side, only narrowly avoiding a statue of Henry Purcell and causing it to wobble dizzily on its plinth.

After Hugo's somewhat theatrical departure, she ascended the stairs once more to her husband's study, where she found him at his desk completely engrossed in a book about flute music at the court of Frederick the Great. Gently, she closed the door and, without a word, crept quietly away.

Peace and tranquillity had once again resumed their reign at Luxbrough House.

♪

Hugo had always taken pride in his use of English and style of writing, whether penning an article for a newspaper, a musical review, or even a letter to a friend; not for him the hackneyed phrase, the soiled verbal hand-me-down of lesser talents. Nevertheless, in describing to Gina his state of mind upon leaving Professor Wetherby's house, only the words 'incandescent with rage' came to mind. He simply could not marshal his thoughts sufficiently to invent an alternative expression with enough vim to do justice to the way he felt upon being so horribly snubbed.

As he had driven back through the village at reckless speed, he was, if not actually 'foaming at the mouth', positively 'shaking with fury'. All the way back to London he was 'beside himself with anger', and even when he finally arrived at the flat at Beacon Court to pour out his soul to Gina, he was very cross indeed.

It took all Gina's soothing, seductive powers to calm him down and several precious glasses of Dom Pérignon.

"You're really rather wonderful when you're angry, Hugo – like a grizzly bear stung by a swarm of bees. So ferocious! I must find ways to enrage you more often."

"Grrrr…"

"Well, perhaps not. Perhaps you'd remind me too much of Frank, and that would never do. No, on second thoughts, I'll just settle for the urbane wit and charm after all."

Even as he made love to Gina, an activity which normally suppressed thought of anything else, one stubborn question kept intruding: how to get his own back on that bastard Wetherby. By what means, he didn't know, but somehow, some day, he would extract his revenge… By God he would!

Too busy paying court to old Dom Pérignon, neither Gina nor Hugo had noticed the figure skulking behind the forest of exotic plants on the balcony outside the drawing room.

After making their way to the bedroom, they had not heard

the same sinister figure stealthily creeping into the flat through the sliding glass doors of the French window which Gina had left open, nor were they conscious of his presence outside the bedroom door listening to them as they made love.

Nor had they heard a thing as the intruder crept away as surreptitiously as he had entered, and by the same route – out onto the balcony, scrambling up onto the flat roof of the apartment block, quickly moving across to the rear and making his way off via the fire escape and the side passageway.

Wednesday 25th May 2005

The Benedictine monastery of San Martino di Roccabella stood on a large rocky outcrop high in the hills on the border between Tuscany and Umbria, overlooking the village of Roccabella. It was a remote and beautiful place, but this did not prevent the tourist coaches from winding their tortuous way up the valley to visit it. The Romanesque Abbey church and the cloister with its famous frescoes depicting scenes from the Nativity were open to the public on Wednesdays and Thursdays from April to September.

Father Gesualdo had quite forgotten that it was a Wednesday as he stepped through the door which led from the monks' refectory to the northern end of the cloister, only to find the place infested by a large party of English sightseers. Father Gesualdo did not like tourists, especially those who arrived by coach. They disturbed the ordered calm of the place.

Retracing his steps a little, he circled the cloister in the other direction, the long way round, until he came to an elaborately carved door through which he passed. The monks' cells now only occupied one wing of the old monastery building due to a decline over the years in the number of vocations, but the unoccupied wing had been converted into a magnificent library, where, at last, the monastery's treasure trove of sacred texts and manuscripts could be properly housed and made available for scholarly inspection and research. It was to the library that Father Gesualdo was intent on making his way. He was the monastery librarian and archivist, and the library was his pride and joy. Many happy hours were spent there each day, only interrupted by the various services in the Abbey church and the need to read his office as the Rule of St Benedict required of him. It was to the very top floor of the library wing that he now climbed. The view from there was quite superb, a view stretching into the far distance of vineyards, olive groves and cypress-clad hills virtually unchanged in centuries.

Unfortunately, however, if you permitted your eye to fall upon the immediate foreground, a corner of the car park was just visible. The modern world had gatecrashed this timeless scene in its brash, vulgar way as it had in so many places. Sure enough, looking out of the window, there was the dreaded English coach, and yet another coach, a Dutch one this time, was just drawing into the park at that very moment.

Father Gesualdo grunted disdainfully, averting his gaze and looking instead towards the reddish-brown roof tiles of the old town of Roccabella and the matchless Italianate landscape beyond. He tried hard to imagine a vision of the Virgin Mary and Child in the centre of the window with a vista of distant mountains behind, as if the window itself framed some Renaissance painting by Perugino or Fra Angelico, but, try as he might, all that he could conjure up was an image of one of the English coach party, a large lady of indeterminate years with untidy hair and blotchy sunburnt arms, wearing a cheap sack-like summer frock and flip-flops – behold, the Blessed Virgin of Basingstoke, the Madonna of the flip-flops!

"Povero me, povero me!" he sighed. Jesus clearly was chiding him for his lack of humility, not to mention the uncharitable feelings he harboured towards the wretched tourists. They did him no real harm, and, doubtless made a valuable contribution to Abbey funds. Ah well, he thought, time to continue with his important work – the cataloguing of the monastery's valuable collections, a labour of love which it would take him many more years of painstaking effort to complete.

Most of the books and manuscripts were, of course, of a sacred nature, but on occasion Father Gesualdo came across a secular work. Only a month before, he had found a first edition of Les Liaisons Dangereuses, the salacious eighteenth-century French novel by Pierre de Laclos, buried beneath a stack of old breviaries. This was sent to a saleroom in Paris for auction… but not before the Prior had caught one of the novice monks, poor little Brother Alfredo, avidly reading it as he squatted to conceal himself behind an ancient cope chest in the Abbey crypt.

Father Gesualdo was currently engaged upon the monastery's extensive collection of medieval psalters, all containing beautifully illuminated lettering and assembled from all over Europe and from different periods: Lombardic, French gothic, Anglo-Saxon, and Celtic, together with some later examples from the Renaissance. As he took a book from the shelf, he accidentally dislodged another volume which came crashing to the floor. Horrified, he put the first one down and gathered up the fallen volume, most concerned in case it had suffered any damage. To his surprise it was not, however, another psalter, but an eighteenth-century printed edition of a musical score; the score of an opera, Il Servitore di Due Padroni by Baldassarre Galuppi, based on Goldoni's play of the same name. How on earth it had got there, nobody would ever know.

The discovery of the Galuppi opera was of course of considerable musical importance in its own right, but a comparison with the Bloomsbury manuscript revealed that, apart from being based on the same play by Goldoni, the music of the Galuppi opera bore no similarity whatever to the one found in London. Therefore, the Bloomsbury opera was quite definitely not a German version of the work of Baldassarre Galuppi.

Friday 15th August 1828

"Well, Vascal, my old friend, I must congratulate you," Signor Rossini said, taking Antoine Vascal by the arm, as together the two of them left the Conservatoire after the premiere performance of Antoine's 'Serenade for Wind Instruments'. "I thought the players really did justice to your charming little piece today."

"Why, thank you my dear sir, it was indeed kind of you to take the time to attend when you must be so busy with your new opera." Antoine knew Rossini's new French opera, Le Comte Ory, was to receive its first performance the following week, and it had been extraordinarily kind of him to take time away from rehearsals to come to his humble concert at the Conservatoire.

A friend of Antoine's wife, Madeleine, had introduced them some years before and Rossini seemed to have taken an instant liking to him, a liking which was entirely reciprocated. Antoine guessed too that, like almost every man who had ever met her, Rossini had a tender spot in his heart for Madeleine. In any event, he always made a point of sending them both tickets for the performance of his operas. Antoine felt very privileged indeed to be able to call such an august person his friend, and flattered too that the great composer had troubled to take an interest in his music.

"Not at all, Vascal. It was indeed a pleasure," Rossini replied.

"And you did not then consider my work utterly worthless, sir?"

"Of course not, my dear fellow. Your Wind Serenata is quite

delightful. I particularly enjoyed the manner in which the notes seemed to scamper after each other like naughty children playing truant. Although, if you will forgive my opinion, it is a piece which would best be played after a good dinner and when the cognac has had ample opportunity to circulate!"

"Oh yes, I am sure you are completely right, Signor Rossini – a good dinner and plenty of cognac!"

"Now, my good friend, I trust you and your charming spouse will be coming to see Le Comte Ory next week."

"Yes, of course we shall."

"Good, good. I hope too that you will both be able to join me for dinner afterwards at La Maison Dorée. The chef tells me that he is preparing a special new dish to be dedicated to me in honour of the occasion – not one, you see, but two compositions to be premiered on the same night!"

Tuesday 31st May 2005

The time of Sandra's appointment with Sir Marcus Lismore had almost arrived. She had finally plucked up the courage to telephone his secretary. Sir Marcus, as an increasingly sought after conductor, was heavily engaged, but after some to-ing and fro-ing, the secretary had managed to find a slot for her in his busy schedule. She was due at his house in Chiswick at 6.30pm that evening. Nervously, she approached the pink Regency villa on the corner of a quiet little street. The directions which the secretary had given her were not difficult to follow and she had arrived there somewhat ahead of time and had walked around the block two or three times. How would she cope if he gave her one of his piercing looks as he had when last they met? Would she give a good account of herself or would she be left speechless and stammering, creating the impression of a silly little provincial girl with ambitions far beyond anything which she would be capable of achieving?

At 6.25pm precisely, she mounted the steps to the front door and rang the bell. The door was opened almost at once by a tall, slim, attractive lady, very smartly dressed.

"Good evening," she said in a very superior accent which Sandra instantly recognised from the telephone. "I'm Griselda Barnett, Sir Marcus's secretary. You must be Miss Grisewood. Do come in. Sir Marcus will be with you shortly."

Sandra was shown into a large drawing room. It was of course an exquisite room, full of exquisite things. Sandra had come to expect everything about Marcus Lismore to be exquisite. But this room was more than just exquisite. If Adam had been there, he would have been able to tell her that it was decorated and furnished in the French Empire style at its most extravagant

As it was, Sandra could only gawp with amazement as she took in her surroundings. There were pictures everywhere.

Classical scenes drawing their inspiration from Greek and Roman antiquity – Anthony meeting Cleopatra, the death of Socrates and so on; heroic scenes of military prowess – cavalrymen in resplendent uniforms, shiny plumed helmets and swirling capes, flashing sabres and cannons belching fire and smoke; semi-erotic paintings – pink, fleshy, nude goddesses transported heavenwards on fluffy white clouds in a powder blue sky, encircled by buzzing little cherubs with naughty faces; voluptuous beauties posing provocatively in elegant Parisian salons or lolling on cushions in exotic Turkish seraglios fanned by turbanned, baggy-trousered eunuchs; jolly scenes of fêtes champêtres – fashionable eighteenth-century society disporting itself in an idealized pastoral setting, drinking, gossiping, flirting, tootling flutes and strumming mandolins, watched over, of course, by more naughty little cherubs peering down from the tops of trees or from behind ivy-wreathed statues of Greek poets and philosophers.

At the opposite end of the room, from where Sandra had entered it, there was a huge marble fireplace with a magnificent neo-baroque gilded mirror above and to the left of the fireplace there was an imposing portrait hung in a well-lit alcove of a figure in a military uniform with gold epaulettes which she was quite sure was supposed to represent Napoleon. In fact, it looked quite similar to a portrait of Napoleon pictured in a book which Adam had recently shown her, and it reminded too her of a film she'd once seen about the battle of Waterloo. At the same time, she felt there was something rather odd about it…Suddenly she realized the portrait bore a striking resemblance to Sir Marcus himself. Sir Marcus Lismore dressed up as Napoleon! Wow!

"My dear Sandra," said Marcus Lismore, who had just quietly entered the room, taking Sandra completely by surprise. "I'm so sorry to have kept you waiting. Please do sit down and make yourself comfortable. I have asked Miss Barnett to bring us some tea."

Sandra sat down.

"I could not help but notice," Sir Marcus continued, "that when I came in you were looking at my pictures. May I ask if you are interested in art?"

"Oh, yes."

"Good, good. An appreciation of fine art is as essential to a truly fulfilling life as music and literature."

The tea arrived, and Griselda poured them each a cup, smiled pleasantly and silently withdrew.

"Now, Sandra," Sir Marcus continued, "down to business. Tell me all about yourself, in particular your musical education and experience."

Sandra told him how she had joined the church choir and how the choirmaster, Mr Peabody, had coached and encouraged her.

She told him all about the evening when he had taken her to the opera in Buxton when her great ambition had taken root. She advised him of her experience with the amateur operatic society and about the singing lessons she attended in Fulham every Wednesday evening with a former music teacher from one of England's great cathedral schools, to whom the good Mr Peabody had kindly provided her with a letter of introduction. She was also, she mentioned, attending evening classes in Italian and German, and her teachers had all declared her accent and pronunciation to be excellent.

"All these things are very good, Sandra, but they are not enough. You need to go up a gear if you really aspire to an operatic career. More teaching and practise will be required, much more… but all this I can help to arrange. It will be hard work. It may well involve you giving up your present job, but it will certainly be worth it in the end, I promise you. You have a quite remarkable natural talent and it will see you through. Now, are you ready to make the necessary sacrifices for the sake of your future?"

"Oh, yes," she said, trembling with excitement as Sir Marcus spoke. 'Oh, yes' were about the only words to which Sandra was able, at that moment, to give coherent utterance.

"Well, my dear, you will be pleased to hear that I have a role in mind for you to which I believe you would be ideally suited. There are others, besides myself, whom you will need to impress, but the final decision usually rests with me. Now, do you feel you are up to the challenge?"

"Oh, yes!"

"Good, good. That's splendid! Now, Sandra, it would give me the greatest pleasure if you would agree to be my guest this evening for dinner at Chez Véronique. My chauffeur will drive you home afterwards."

"Oh, yes… oh, yes, I'd love to!" Sandra replied, overjoyed at the prospect of dinner at last at the famous Chez Véronique. How she would enjoy telling Adam where she'd been!

"Are you sure Adam won't mind?"

"Oh, yes… oh, I mean no!"

Sir Marcus smiled.

"Good, good, then that's settled."

The posh Griselda appeared once more on cue.

"Chez Véronique phoned, Sir Marcus. They're very busy this evening, but they've found you a table."

"Well, of course they have, they always have a table at Chez Véronique for Sir Marcus Lismore and his guests!"

Thursday 2nd June 2005

"The barbarians are at the gate, Alice!" trumpeted Professor Justin Wetherby.

"Nowadays," he continued, "yob culture is in the ascendant. It is all pervasive, fuelled by a diet of football, lager, sexual licentiousness, and the worship of worthless celebrities. Loss of deference has led to a loss of civility. Everywhere, civilization is in retreat and vulgarity triumphant. I blame the internet. The trouble today is that lack of culture is no bar to advancement as once it used to be. Any spiv with a bit of cheek and a computer can do almost anything now. They have money, and they travel, too!"

It was not the first time that Mrs Wetherby had heard her husband indulge in this somewhat disjointed little rant. She referred to it as 'The-End-of-Civilization-as-We-Know-It-Speech'. Mercifully, whether true or not, he had ceased generally to regale their dinner party guests with it any more. It tended these days to be confined to the back of a taxi on the way to Heathrow, as indeed it was on this occasion. It was the thought of standing in the check-in queue with all sorts of people that brought it on, she supposed.

He would be perfectly normal again, she told herself calmly, as soon as they were safely ensconced at his favourite hotel, near the cathedral, in Vienna, whither they were bound that morning.

Vienna was the venue of an academic conference, held annually each summer in a different European city, on some aspect or theme of Western culture. This time the subject was 'The Influence of the Arts on Social Habits and Customs in the Age of the Enlightenment'. Professor Wetherby was to deliver a lecture entitled 'The Growing Importance of Opera as Public Entertainment'. He always looked forward to these conferences. They were a good opportunity to renew old acquaintances, and the task of preparing for his lecture was scarcely an arduous one for him.

The check-in queue at Heathrow was not as daunting as Alice Wetherby had feared it might be, the flight left on time and there were no overtly obnoxious passengers or rowdy children on board. Soon, Wetherby's expression assumed an air of benign, slightly bemused detachment, his usual default mode when confronted with the public en masse. As Alice had predicted, he became completely his normal self again almost as soon as they arrived at the hotel.

Moreover, it seemed the day could only get better. As they were waiting at reception for a porter to take their bags up to the room, another English couple arrived whom Justin instantly recognised as his old friend Professor Edwin Bleddoes and his wife Joyce. He knew, of course, that Bleddoes would be attending the conference, but had no idea that he and his wife would be staying at the same hotel. What an unexpected pleasure!

Following a brief rest in their rooms to refresh themselves after the journey, they set out for a short stroll together along the Kärtner Strasse, stopping off for a coffee and a Sachertorte at one of the cafés en route.

"Remind me, Edwin, what is it that you are to talk about?"

"I am to deliver a short paper, 'The Grand Tour – its Social and Cultural Significance.'"

"How very interesting."

"Well, it was frankly a little difficult to find anything very original to say on such a well-worn topic, but then quite by chance a few weeks ago I was sent for inspection an old diary which had been found at a solicitors' office in Shropshire in a family deed box belonging to a recently deceased client…"

"A diary?"

"Yes, it was the diary of a young woman who had accompanied her husband on the Grand Tour during the 1780s. The young lady – Eleanor Foxley by name – was a most observant and intelligent person and a good writer, too. The diary is most illuminating and will, in my opinion, come to be regarded as important source material in this area. It covers all of the period during which the couple were travelling in Europe and contains, I can tell you, some fascinating new information as well as revealing insights on the social customs and attitudes of the time. It is really quite a significant discovery."

"How fortuitous that it should have come to light just in time for your lecture!"

"Yes, indeed, and in fact there is something in it which I know will be of great interest to you, Justin."

"Really?"

"Yes. I must confess that I have only just finished reading the diary; otherwise, I would have been in touch with you before. Most of the diary covers the outward leg of the couple's tour as far as their arrival in Sicily, which provided quite enough material for my talk. However, the later pages, which I only just got round to reading in the last few days, cover the return leg of the journey, travelling via central Europe, in the course of which Eleanor mentions a visit to the Palace of Esterházy, where she met Joseph

Haydn, who of course was the resident Kapellmeister and court composer. Indeed, there is quite lengthy description of the visit, and it is this part, Justin, that you really must read.

"Splendid. I will look forward to it. Have you brought this diary with you?"

"Well, of course I didn't think it would be right to take the original diary here to Vienna, but I arranged for extracts to be copied to bring with me as part of the material for my talk, and knowing that you would be here at the conference, I also had those later pages which include the Esterházy visit, copied. I could bring them to your room this evening before dinner, if you'd like."

Later, as Alice was enjoying a long soak in the bath, Justin Wetherby sat reading the extracts from Eleanor's diary which Edwin Bleddoes had delivered to him as promised. There were some interesting entries concerning the Foxleys' arrival in Vienna: people they had met, concerts they had attended, and so forth. Finally, he came to the Esterházy visit. It seemed that Eleanor's husband, Sir Charles Foxley, was distantly related to Prince Nikolaus Esterházy through a well-connected cousin, by whose kind offices an invitation to visit Esterházy Palace had been arranged. Wetherby read on:

Wednesday, the 20th day of August 1783
We arrived late at Esterházy after a most wearisome journey in very warm weather. My first sight of the palace, as our coach approached, quite silenced my normal busy tongue. Poor Charles thought me to be suffering a fit of the vapours on account of the heat, and attempted to fan me with his hat. However, as I tried in vain to explain, it was the view of the palace itself that had robbed me of speech, so grand is it in its majestic size but so intimate in the exquisite detail of its ornamentation. Of course, the great

palace of Versailles was, I knew, the inspiration for its construction so that I should not have been at all surprised, but I found myself nevertheless quite overcome.

The room in the guests' quarters to which we were shown by the Prince's steward is most agreeable in every respect, but we had little opportunity for rest and barely time to change from our travelling clothes before the evening's entertainment began.

The entertainment took the form of a play for puppets and it was held in the marionette theatre which lies opposite the opera house which has been newly rebuilt. The marionette theatre was constructed, I understand, to resemble in its exterior design the old opera house which was destroyed in a fire some years ago. Inside, the theatre is like a grotto with its walls and niches covered in many coloured stones and sea shells which magically reflect the light, and all the puppets are most beautifully made and dressed. The play this evening was 'L'Assedio di Gibilterra', concerning the siege of Gibraltar, for which the most sublime incidental music was provided by Kapellmeister Haydn. Poor Charles, though, to my eternal mortification, contrived to fall asleep almost as soon as the performance began.

After the play, we attended a wonderful banquet prepared for the prince's guests, at which I was privileged to meet the great Joseph Haydn himself…

Wetherby continued to read with mounting interest. When Alice eventually emerged from the bathroom, she was treated to the unusual spectacle of her husband doing what appeared to be a little jig around the room.

"What on earth are you doing, Justin? What's the matter – are you ill?"

"No, no, not ill at all. I'm rejoicing!"

"What do you mean 'rejoicing'?" Alice asked, still unconvinced that he was not suffering some form of mental aberration or fit.

"The matter is resolved. I was right!"

"Right? Right about what?"

"Mozart did complete the opera The Servant of Two Masters – it's all here in the diary!"

Without reading it all word for word, Justin explained to Alice broadly what Eleanor had written about her visit in August 1783 to the Palace of Esterházy and about Joseph Haydn, the Court Kapellmeister.

Eleanor had been introduced to Haydn, with whom she had enjoyed a most interesting conversation. It was conducted largely in Italian, a language which Haydn, who had not then mastered English, spoke well and in which Eleanor, with her musical ear, had acquired a reasonable fluency during her stay in Italy.

Eleanor had, during the course of this conversation, asked Haydn if he had any plans to compose a new opera as she had much enjoyed the music which he had composed for the puppet play performed that evening. Haydn told her that he had indeed intended to write an opera based on Goldoni's play Il Servitore di Due Padroni, but Prince Galitzin, who had recently visited Esterházy, had advised him that Mozart had just completed a German opera based upon the same play, and hoped to stage it by Easter of the following year.

With some regret, Haydn had therefore abandoned the idea of writing his own opera based on the play as it would inevitably be compared invidiously with that of Mozart.

It was game, set and match so far as Wetherby was concerned – proof positive that Mozart had indeed written the opera based on Goldoni's play.

What else could the Bloomsbury find be, if not Mozart's lost score?

A press conference in Vienna was hurriedly arranged for the very next day, Friday 3rd June, at which Professor Wetherby proudly broke the news which was widely reported in the media throughout Europe and America.

Prince Galitzin, the Russian ambassador in Vienna, was a friend and patron of Mozart and must be regarded as a reliable source, though one does not know whether he learnt about the opera directly from Mozart or through another friend. The information from Galitzin that Mozart had completed his opera, as some commentators were quick to point out, did not amount to first-hand evidence, in the sense that there was no confirmation directly from Mozart himself and no evidence that anyone had actually viewed the completed score.

There was no evidence, indeed, that the opera had been staged, whether by Easter of 1784 or at all, in Vienna or elsewhere. Wetherby contended that, as 1784 was an incredibly busy year for Mozart, mainly with subscription concerts for new piano concertos, he simply wouldn't have had the time to rehearse and stage the work. When he did have time available he had probably moved on to newer projects, leaving the opera unperformed.

But what did *completed* really mean? Perhaps, Mozart was being a little elastic with the truth, as at times he was. Maybe he had only written a little down in a formal score. Possibly the rest of the work had simply been sketched out roughly in his mind. Much of Mozart's music was composed in his head before being committed to the pages of a score. Mozart was often in debt and there was the constant need to reassure creditors and benefactors.

Even if Mozart had indeed properly completed the opera, as the evidence on the face of it suggested, there was still no real proof to confirm the authenticity of the Bloomsbury manuscript as a copy of the original score.

Nevertheless, the tide of opinion had now generally turned in Wetherby's favour. No other composer in the eighteenth or nineteenth century had been known to write an opera based on Goldoni's play The Servant of Two Masters other than Galuppi, whose score had recently been found in Italy and was not the same as the Bloomsbury score. The other most likely contender, Joseph Haydn, was now out of the running. It was known without doubt that Mozart certainly intended to write such an opera, and now here was cogent evidence that he had done so. The dates also fitted well. The evidence that Mozart had started the opera derived from a letter to his father written in February 1783. The opera could well have been completed by August of that year, when Eleanor had visited Esterházy and had her interesting conversation with Haydn. Mozart was a fast worker. Everybody agreed that the music in the Bloomsbury score was of outstanding quality. Who but Mozart could have written it? There was also the fact, of course, that Wetherby was a leading Mozart scholar who spoke with considerable authority.

A few academics, like Raymond Digby, still considered the evidence inconclusive, but the majority were now inclined to accept Wetherby's attribution of the opera to Mozart.

The final breakthrough had caused something of a sensation, and it was later announced that the opera would be performed during the following year at the Royal Opera House to mark the 250th anniversary of Mozart's birth.

Tuesday 7th June 2005

After hearing the latest news from Wetherby's press conference in Vienna, even Hugo had come to the conclusion that he was probably right, but that did not stop him from hastily drafting a sarcastic article pouring scorn on the whole idea. But he had decided, in the end, not to submit it, realising that it would make he appear ill-humoured and churlish. It now seemed that most people wanted to believe the Bloomsbury score was a genuine Mozart. He would just have to find some other way of getting his own back on the old swine. Perhaps there was some skeleton in Wetherby's cupboard which he could expose. It didn't seem likely though. On the face of it, the man appeared to have enjoyed an exemplary career, and to have led an entirely blameless life – the bastard.

Lisa had flown off to Rome with an old school friend for a few days of serious shopping, a welcome break from the preparations for the wedding which was due to take place on Saturday the 25th of the month, and Gina was spending a few days with her parents in Herefordshire.

Hugo was bored.

He had even considered a visit to the divorcee next door at number 7B, who had moved in only recently and whom Lisa had invited over for drinks with some of the other neighbours just a few days before. What was her name? Something beginning with M? Maria, Martha? No, Muriel. That was it – Muriel. She was not a great beauty, it was true, but she had fantastic legs, absolutely fantastic… and she was gagging for it. No doubt about it. He could tell from the way she had looked at him during the drinks party. On the other hand, it was perhaps a little too close for comfort, even for Hugo, who revelled in taking risks. Also, there were those jerky hand movements and her nervous gushing mode of speech – indications, Hugo considered, of a neurotic type of woman, the sort that often spelt trouble.

The rampaging forces of lust skirmished briefly with the disciplined troops of common sense but the latter, after a valiant tussle on the part of the former, finally prevailed. He would simply have to give Muriel a miss. Shame! The legs were damn good. He might, though, he thought, have to reconsider the matter if no better idea presented itself by the evening.

Switching on the radio, he planted himself with a reluctant sigh in his favourite armchair.

"And now," the programme presenter intoned in that special Radio 3 sort of voice, "for a rarely heard piece of nineteenth-century wind music, a Wind Serenade in D Major by Antoine Vascal. Not much is known of Vascal's origins but he spent the greater part of his long life in Paris. A friend of Rossini and Gounod, both of whom mention him with affection in their letters, he was a pianist of some repute, though noted more for his capacity for lyrical charm than any great virtuosity. Vascal also composed many pieces of what might loosely be described as 'light salon music', of which his Wind Serenade is a good example. It is played on this recording by the Elysian Wind Ensemble, and is in five short movements…"

The music was pleasant enough in a frothy sort of way, good background stuff, but insufficiently absorbing to occupy Hugo's entire attention. He had read everything interesting there was to read in the newspaper, and, searching for something else to do, picked up the book of memoirs he had bought in Paris by Victor Chavigny. He had only read about half of it so far. It was one of those books one likes to dip into from time to time in a spare moment. The memoirs were a bit of a mixed bag, varying between accounts of historical events and Chavigny's impressions of literary and artistic figures of the day, interspersed with personal reminiscences. The latter happily included some deliciously erotic episodes of the sort Hugo much enjoyed – Dear old Monsieur Lapiteau had not let him down. He never did.

A whole chapter was devoted to Chavigny's visit as a seventeen-year-old youth to Napoleon's tomb at Les Invalides, where the great monster had been reburied in 1840, including a long piece concerning the speculation that he may in fact have escaped from St Helena to Italy, and that the remains in the tomb belonged to someone else altogether. In a more personal vein, there was a charming description of a ride with his father on the new railway between Paris and Saint-Germain-en-Laye. More entertaining still, though, was a racy passage describing in the most intimate detail young Victor's seduction of a half-caste Mauritian lady who was, it seemed, also Baudelaire's mistress. There were interesting observations on the overthrow of the newly restored monarchy in 1848 and the coup d'état which brought Napoleon's nephew to power.

The chapter he was in the middle of reading had begun with a rather turgid assessment of the female writer, Amantine Dupin, better known as George Sand as she chose to call herself, her relationship with Chopin, and her lack of conformity with the generally accepted gender roles of the day. The serious stuff soon mercifully gave way to a superbly titillating tale of a three-to-a-bed romp involving Chavigny and two young ballerinas, later joined by their dancing mistress and her pet snake. Splendid stuff!

He had nearly come to the end of the chapter when the doorbell rang. Rising to his feet, he put the book down on the arm of his chair and went to answer the door, wondering who it might be.

♪

Should she, or shouldn't she?

That was the question in poor Muriel's mind. Should she go next door and invite Hugo Belcher round for dinner in the evening or not?

She knew that Lisa, his fiancée, was away in Rome. She had said she was going when Muriel had been in for drinks the other evening, and that morning she had seen the taxi arrive and Lisa getting into it with her suitcase. Hugo was therefore presumably alone in the house.

Would it not be an act of kindness to ask him round for dinner? Hugo would probably only go out and get a takeaway to eat all alone by himself. Would he not be pleased of the company and a decent healthy meal, too? Was this not what good neighbours were for? she tried to persuade herself.

No, Muriel! her alter ego admonished sternly. That's just self-serving nonsense, and you know it. You want to invite Hugo because you find him wildly attractive, and you saw the way he was looking at your legs. Your female intuition tells you that you might be in with a chance. You're already fantasising about what it would be like to go to bed with him, aren't you?

Stop it, stop it! Why on earth should she assume, Muriel replied to herself crossly, that he's the sort of man who would seduce her, or rather allow himself to be seduced, after only having met her once? Besides he would be betraying his fiancée…

Hugo has wavy hair. So?

Remember what your mother always used to say: "Beware of men with wavy hair!" Your ex-husband had wavy hair and look at the sort of man he turned out to be. Your female antennae are telling you that Hugo is a bad man, a very bad man.

All right, she admitted it. She suspected that Hugo was indeed a rogue who would take ruthless advantage of her, but, if she was honest, she'd always preferred bad men – so much more exciting! And right now, she really wanted a man like that to do lots of very bad things to her. Why not? She deserved a bit of real pleasure didn't she after all she'd been through?

Silence. Not a word from the alter ego.

Oh, I suppose I'd better not, Muriel thought sadly.

No, for God's sake, why ever not? She bloody well would invite him. So there!

Suppressing visions of her mother's wagging finger and of poor Lisa's sweet innocent face, Muriel opened her front door and stepped into the street, only to retreat again immediately and run upstairs to her bedroom taking two steps at a time.

A few seconds rummaging in the wardrobe produced what she was looking for: the very short black leather skirt she had bought in the new year sales and had never before dared to wear. Would she dare now? Yes, she jolly well would.

God, it really was very, very short, she thought, rather nervously, as she put it on. Hastily, she applied some make-up and a little of the powerful musky scent which her sister had given her for her birthday, and stood back to look at the result in the mirror…. Jesus! She looked like some cheap tart, and smelt like one, too. But that was rather the point wasn't it? It provided her with a kind of emotional defence. It would not be her, the real Muriel, who succumbed – hopefully – to Hugo's seductive charms, but this other, tarted-up Muriel woman, so that whatever happened, she, Muriel, could distance herself from it… sort of… in her mind. It would not be her fault. Not really.

Determined to retain the firm resolve she had battled against all the odds to summon up, she hurried downstairs again and out into the street before any new thoughts could form in her mind and blow her off course.

A few brief strides brought her to Hugo's front door, which she found to be slightly ajar. Good! That obviously meant he was at home.

She rang the bell. No immediate answer.

"Mr Belcher… er… Hugo," she called out a little uncertainly, her resolution already beginning to waver. Still no answer.

Bravely she pushed the door and stepped into the hallway, calling Hugo's name again, doing her best to sound positive and friendly. Almost immediately, she stumbled against something on the floor and nearly tripped.

The something with which her foot had connected was Hugo's bloody corpse. It was a truly terrible sight. He had been stabbed several times in the chest and abdomen and his throat had been cut.

Poor Muriel fainted with shock. She would require many months of expensive professional counselling to overcome the dreadful trauma she had suffered.

Later that day, Detective Chief Inspector Stan Gormley of the Metropolitan Police, speaking on the local radio news, appealed for witnesses who might have been in the vicinity of Wellington Mews at about 11.30 that morning.

The police, he said, were keeping an open mind, but "this appalling incident bore all the hallmarks of a drug-related crime."

To begin with, there was the nature of the attack – a violent frenzied assault with a knife. "The recent increase in knife attacks," the Chief Inspector continued, "has become one of the issues around drug crime causing grave concern to the police in London."

Secondly, Mr Belcher's wallet was missing, and all the cupboard doors and drawers in the house were open and the place was in a mess, obviously indicating theft.

Lastly, a used syringe had been discovered just inside the hallway. It had been sent for analysis, but the Chief Inspector strongly suspected it would be found to contain traces of "an unlawful substance".

It was not difficult, in DCI Gormley's opinion, to envisage what had obviously occurred: the offender would have been in the neighbourhood, most likely looking for cars to break into. As he passed the cottage, he would have looked through a window, seen that someone was at home and rang the doorbell. When Mr

Belcher opened it, he would have threatened him with a knife and demanded money or valuables to sell, cash that he needed to buy drugs. Mr Belcher, it must be assumed, would have resisted or tried to slam the door and the offender had lashed out with his knife with fatal effect. He would then have quickly stolen what he could and made off.

Members of the public, the Chief Inspector warned, should be very careful before opening the door to strangers.

A young man in a baseball cap had been witnessed loitering near the scene at about the relevant time, and the police would particularly appreciate any further information from anyone in the area who might have seen a person answering this description.

Chief Inspector Gormley was quite confident that with the public's help an arrest would be made very soon.

Wednesday 8th June 2005

Frank's car drew up in the driveway in front of Syracuse Lodge after the long drive back from Heathrow Airport where he had gone that morning to pick up his daughter, Lisa. She and her friend had returned early from their shopping trip to Rome on the first available flight after Frank had phoned the evening before with the dreadful news of Hugo's death. They were met in the hallway by Maria, Frank's housekeeper, and Frank asked her to go up with Lisa to her bedroom, help her with her things and see that she went to bed. He would phone the doctor to ask him to prescribe a sedative. Maria advised him that Toni Belcanto was waiting to see him in his study.

Frank was expecting him and had noticed his car parked in the drive when he arrived.

Antonio Belcanto, or Toni as he was usually called, was Frank's second cousin. He had come to England in his twenties and, though not quite in the same league as Frank, had also built a successful business career, with fingers in a number of pies in the Manchester area. He and Frank had always been very close.

A few of the Sicilian community, of which Frank and Toni were part, might on occasion be less than scrupulous in their business dealings or perhaps not entirely honest with the taxman, but it would be a myth to suppose that they all had some association with the Mafia or the local underworld. Indeed, the great majority led perfectly respectable, blameless lives. Frank too, like his father before him, had always steered clear of any dubious connection of this kind.

However, in Toni's case it was a different story. His business enterprises were entirely above board, but he maintained contacts with certain people, both in Sicily and the UK, people who were rather less than respectable and blameless, people with links to the Mafia or organised crime. Toni would sometimes do favours for these people – usually of a money-laundering nature – and sometimes he would receive favours in return.

Frank was aware of these associations, though he took care to distance himself from them. On a few occasions over the years, though, he had called upon Toni for help in resolving a problem where every other solution had been tried and failed. There was, for example, the manager who Frank suspected had his hand in the till – he was savagely beaten up in the road outside his home by two large men in black balaclavas in front of his horrified wife. There was a business rival who was trying to pinch one of Belcanto's best customers – his offices were comprehensively trashed. Then, there was the neighbour who had had the effrontery to lodge an objection to a planning application Frank had made for a minor extension to Syracuse Lodge – the tyres of his new Range Rover were slashed and a load of builders' waste was deposited on his front lawn. All of them, in the time-honoured phrase, 'got the message'.

It was to Toni that Frank had turned for help again, back in April, in connection with a very personal matter.

Ever since the time Frank had arrived unexpectedly and found Gina in bed quite early in the evening with a bottle of champagne, he sensed instinctively that something was wrong. It was the same instinct, so valuable to him in business, which told him when a deal was going sour. For a good while he had tried to exclude from his mind the dreadful thoughts and imaginings that came upon him. He tried telling himself that there was no evidence of anything and that he must be mistaken, but the thoughts kept insidiously creeping back, finally driving him to distraction. Eventually, he had picked up the phone to Toni and asked him round for a drink.

When Frank had unburdened himself of his suspicions, Toni promised he would do what he could to help. He had a 'friend' in London who owed him a favour. A watchful eye would be kept on Gina's apartment and her comings and goings.

Toni contacted Sandro, a gangland creature heavily involved in drug smuggling and people trafficking operating behind a façade of legitimate businesses. He would put one of his most reliable young men on the job.

It had taken much longer than Toni had hoped to come up with an answer, partly because Sandro's man, Carmelo, couldn't be watching Gina all day and night, and some days he had other assignments to perform.

Gradually, however, a picture began to emerge. It became clear, after a while, that there was a regular rather posh-looking male visitor to Beacon Court, but there were other regular visitors too, and Carmelo was usually too far away to see precisely which of the entry phone buttons were pressed. He had not wanted to question the caretaker about visitors in case it got back to Gina, nor had he wanted to stand too close or spy through binoculars in case he was observed. However, he had managed to get near enough one evening to see that the posh visitor pressed the top button of the entry phone, the button for the penthouse apartment where Gina lived. He had managed to do the same again on two later occasions and each time the same man was seen to press the same button.

Gina was usually picked up in the mornings by her friend and business partner to go to work at her art gallery, but one day she left home alone in the Mercedes, and Carmelo decided to follow her on his motorbike. She had not driven far before she turned into a cobbled mews and stopped outside one of the cottages. A man came out and got into the car. It was the same posh figure who regularly visited Beacon Court and pressed Gina's entry phone button.

This was, in fact, the day when Gina and Hugo had visited Hugo's mother and spent the night at the Pemberton Arms. Carmelo managed to take a good photograph of the man, which Sandro promptly emailed to Toni. Toni had only met Hugo once, at Lisa's engagement party, but he recognised him immediately. Of course, Hugo's visits to Gina might be quite innocent, but Toni was sure in his own mind what was going on. However, before he approached Frank, he wanted Sandro's man to do one more thing – he wanted him somehow to get inside the apartment when Hugo was there alone with Gina. Except for the ground floor, all the apartments had small terraces or balconies with French windows giving access to them, and Carmelo had noticed that many of the residents routinely left these windows open, especially if it was a warm day. He couldn't see Gina's penthouse apartment very clearly from the street as it was too high up, but he betted Gina would do the same. On the day Hugo had returned to Gina's apartment after his abortive visit to interview Professor Wetherby,

Carmelo had thus duly gained entry via the flat roof of the apartment block, and any remaining doubt was removed. Toni arranged to meet Frank to give him the bad news.

Frank predictably flew into a rage and stamped around the room, cursing, throwing things and upsetting the furniture. Eventually, having calmed down a little, he slumped into a chair, holding his head in his hands.

"Toni," he said, finally looking up and managing to pull himself together, "I want him gone… out of my life completely."

"You mean, you want him frightened off?"

"No, Toni, I want him dead!"

"Dead?!"

"Yes, fucking dead!"

Next day, Toni had travelled to London to meet Sandro. Sandro couldn't get the job done himself, but he knew someone who could, a specialist. He would get this man to contact Toni as soon as possible. Sandro warned that it would be expensive, but Toni hastened to assure him that money was no object.

Some days later, a man called at Toni's home in the evening. He introduced himself simply as Salvatore and he was, he said, the person Sandro had told him to expect. He was a distinguished-looking man and he spoke very softly with just a trace of an Italian accent. Toni noted how elegantly dressed he was and was impressed with his businesslike manner. Indeed, it was true that Salvatore ran a very efficient business. Like Frank and Toni, he understood the importance of good customer service, tight cost control, and a coherent business plan embracing tough but achievable targets – though target had a somewhat ambiguous meaning so far as Salvatore's business was concerned, and he generally preferred to talk in terms of business goals.

Toni gave him all the details he needed to know about Hugo: a copy of the photograph, the address where Hugo resided with

Lisa, and the important fact that, being freelance, he would be on his own at home for at least part of each day when Lisa was out at work. Payment terms were discussed and agreed – Frank had given him carte blanche to do the necessary deal. Salvatore told him that he had a lot of work on at present, but would get one of his operatives onto the matter as soon as possible.

Just before Toni went out for lunch on the 7th June, he received a phone call. A voice said, "This is a message from Salvatore – the goods you ordered in London have now been delivered."

There was a report of Hugo's murder on the local radio news in London and it was widely covered later in both the local and national press.

"So, the job's done, then," Frank said when they were alone in Frank's study.

"Yes, that motherfucker got what he deserved."

Toni had just managed to stop himself saying "mother-in-law fucker" as a sort of joke; Frank might not consider it in the best of taste, he thought. Besides, Gina was only Lisa's stepmother and in any case the bastard had got what was coming to him before the wedding had actually taken place… Grazie a Dio!

"And there's no way that this could get back to you or me?"

"No way at all, Frank. It was made to look like a drug-related crime – you know, someone trying to get hold of money or stuff to sell to pay for his drug habit, holds up Hugo with a knife, Hugo resists and gets stabbed… The police bought the whole thing."

"Good, good. Well, I suppose you'll want the balance of the money to pay the guy off?"

"Yeah, someone's coming to collect it tomorrow."

"It's all ready for you in £50 notes as arranged in that suitcase by the desk there – take it when you go."

"Thanks, Frank."

"Like a glass of champagne?"

"Thanks, I'd love one."

"Toni," Frank continued, as he poured out the drinks, "I'm very grateful to you for everything you've done. Is there anything I can do for you in return?"

"Well, Frank, perhaps there is. You know my boy Joe has always had a bit of a thing going for Lisa – you couldn't put in a good word with her, could you, Frank? I mean when she's feeling a little better, obviously… It would be nice to see them walking out together, don't you think?"

"Do you know, Toni, that's a very good idea. 'Course I'll say something to Lisa. Joe's a good boy. It would be the best thing for Lisa right now."

Frank was quite genuinely enthusiastic. Toni's boy, Giuseppe Belcanto, Joe as he was called now, was a nice young man; he'd done well at college, qualified as an accountant, and now worked for his father. One day, too, he would inherit the business. He came from the right stock and, if they got married, Lisa wouldn't even have to change her name. Perfect! In fact, there would be no 'ifs' about it. They would be married – Lisa would just bloody well do what her father told her this time, and no argument!

♪

Hugo, however, had not been the only one to have been playing around off-field.

Frank had met Suzie some six months before at a nightclub in Manchester where she worked as a hostess. He had asked her out and not much later they began an affair, though she was hardly much older than his daughter Lisa. The club had strict rules prohibiting staff from going out on dates with patrons and when it was discovered that this had happened, Suzie got the sack, whereupon Frank employed her as his personal secretary. Soon afterwards, he fixed her up in a cosy little flat not far from his office. It was a most convenient arrangement.

Being honest with himself, he found Suzie much easier to get along with than Gina. Gina's sophistication, witty conversation, and social poise made him acutely aware of his own shortcomings, with the result that, in spite of his great wealth and the force of his personality, he was often made to feel inferior in her presence. Suzie, by contrast, never made him feel that way. She may not have been a classy beauty like Gina, but she was a very sexy young woman and certainly knew how to please a man.

Frank showered Suzie with expensive gifts and on a few occasions had taken her with him on business trips abroad. By coincidence, on one such occasion in Milan they had stayed at the very same luxury hotel where Katie, the trainee solicitor, had stayed under somewhat similar circumstances. She might be a bimbo, but if so, like Katie, Suzie was very clever at using her bimbo-ish attractions to get exactly what she wanted.

But what was Frank to do about Gina in the light of her affair with Hugo? That was the question. His initial reaction was that he should hurry down to London, give her damn good beating and throw her out in the street. But he didn't want to leave Lisa on her own, and as the days passed, wiser counsels prevailed.

If it became clear that he had found out about Gina's affair with Hugo, his untimely death soon afterwards might arouse suspicions, no matter how it had been made to look. It would be uncomfortable if the police started sniffing around – who knows what they might dig up?

In any event, he would prefer the affair with Hugo to remain a secret. If people came to know about it, it would make him look a fool. Nobody with any personal pride wants to be shown up as a cuckold.

No, the answer was for him to ask Gina for a divorce because there was now another woman in his life, which after all was true.

He would offer her a generous settlement in place of the pre-nuptial agreement. This would involve paying her a substantial upfront capital sum and agreeing to write off the loan he had made to the art gallery. It would be a clean break.

Plainly Gina had married him for money. Well, now she would have plenty of it and no ongoing commitment to him. She might be a bitch, but she was a clever bitch. She would know a good deal when she saw one. He was quite sure that she would accept.

Of course, he bitterly regretted that he had ever met Gina in the first place, and even more aggrieved at the way in which she had betrayed him. The fact that he had also cheated on her didn't, of course, enter into the equation.

The trick when faced with a difficult situation is to extricate yourself from it as advantageously as possible, and Frank was very good at doing that. Indeed, it was one of the secrets of his success as a businessman. Besides, he reasoned, perhaps in this gloomy dark cloud there was a silver, if not in fact a gold, lining. The end result of Gina's affair with Hugo, after all, was that Lisa would be saved from a rotten marriage, and he would be spared a smarmy, lying bastard for a son-in-law. Benissimo!

Friday 28th September 1849

A horse-drawn cab loomed into sight through the misty twilight of a late September evening in Paris, clopping and clattering along the street until the cab driver reined in the horses, bringing the vehicle to a shuddering halt alongside an elderly man waiting by the roadside. The horses were a little frisky, and it was a struggle to keep them still as the old fellow heaved himself up aboard with difficulty. It was some four years before work began on Baron

Haussman's ambitious building plans, under which large parts of Paris would be restructured and the city we know today created.

The waiting passenger was 'old' Antoine Vascal, known in another life as Antonin Vasylicek. Very old indeed he was for a man of his time, but despite the ravages of age one could still detect the vestiges of a handsome face, a twinkle in the eye, a trace of life's sparkle undimmed. He bade the cabbie a cheery good evening and they set off at a brisk trot, while Antoine happily hummed to himself the bird-catcher's song from The Magic Flute.

He was on his way to the Café Racine, a hostelry in a little corner of old Montmartre – a quiet, unassuming sort of place, quite unlike the great bustling cafés and brasseries of the Belle Époque later to be found on the Grands Boulevards. However, on the last Friday of every month, it came to life, animated by the monthly meeting of the Societé Racine.

The Societé Racine, so called after the place they met and in memory of the famous dramatist, was an informal gathering of artists, writers, musicians and intellectuals, numbering many illustrious names amongst its members. Antoine counted it a great honour to have been asked to join such a distinguished company, and rarely missed a meeting. He was under no illusion, though, that his role in the proceedings, like that of Hugo at Sheridan's Restaurant, was essentially to lighten the mood after the serious debates and discussions of the evening, to smooth any ruffled feathers, to tell tales, to amuse, to entertain… in short to bring the evening to a happy conclusion.

As was the custom, a 'president' was elected at each meeting, and it was his privilege to choose a subject for discussion.

On the evening in question, the chosen proposition was: 'A masterpiece can only be the creation of a genius – true or false?'

Were those beautiful early altarpiece triptychs found in Italian churches masterpieces? If so, were the often-anonymous artists all geniuses, then? Or did they derive their inspiration from some form of collective genius or perhaps they were mere ciphers in the realization of God's own work?

Surely the Symphonie Fantastique was a masterpiece, but was Berlioz then a genius too, fit to rank alongside Bach, Haydn, Mozart and Beethoven?

On the other hand, who but a person of Shakespeare's genius could have written Hamlet?

If someone was a genius, did it automatically follow that all his works were masterpieces? How many masterpieces would someone need to create in order to be considered a genius in the first place? If only one or two works were masterpieces, but the rest were not, then perhaps this would imply that their creator was not a genius after all, which would in turn prove the proposition false… or would it?

What was a masterpiece, anyway? What indeed was the nature of genius? And so on, and so on…

The wine flowed and the arguments raged back and forth amongst the assembled company without reaching any conclusion.

Old Antoine caught the eye of the President of the evening.

"Yes, Antoine?"

"May I be permitted to say a few words, Monsieur President?"

"Of course, you may. I think it is high time for one of your little stories. Is it some delicious piece of gossip? Has some lady been foolish enough perhaps to confide in you some secret of the boudoir? Or is it some outrageous jest, some wicked banter with which you wish to entertain us?"

"No, I'm sorry to disappoint you, Monsieur President et Mes chers confrères, it is none of those things."

"What is it then, Antoine?"

"For once, Monsieur President, I have a little story which may perhaps contribute in some small way to the discussion this evening."

"Mon dieu! Pray speak."

"When I left Prague, the city of my birth, for England, all those years ago, I took with me the manuscript of an opera score and libretto, which had been found in an old house near the Charles Bridge. How I came by it is a long story and need not detain us now."

"I'm sure, though, it would be a story worthy of the telling, like all your stories, Antoine, no doubt involving a woman – but what was this opera called and who was the composer?"

"Well, the opera was called The Servant of Two Masters. It was in German, based on a translation of a play by Goldoni, and according to the title page, it was written by Mozart."

"Mozart?!"

"That was plain nonsense, of course, as I discovered for myself when I eventually came to study the score. It was largely a wretched hotchpotch of arias and duets cobbled together from other works, mainly ones, I recognized, by Mysliviček, an older compatriot of mine who went to work in Italy. All the music had been horribly desecrated in the composer's vain attempts to adapt it to the plot. In fact, it is an insult to the art of composing to refer to the man as a composer at all. A village bandmaster could have made a better job of it."

"Did you ever discover who this composer, this fellow, actually was, then?" someone asked.

"I discovered that another émigré from my native country, whom I chanced upon here in Paris, told me that a music student called Lasek had been trying to pass off an opera score as a lost work by Mozart. I assume that he wrote the opera score, but who wrote the German libretto and how it came into his possession remain a mystery. However, he had hawked the score around a number of music publishers in Prague, all to no avail. No one was taken in, of course. I could recall nothing of this myself but this émigré, whom I met, happened to have worked at one of the publishing houses which this rogue Lasek had approached, and this is how he came to hear of it. He couldn't remember the name of the opera, but was able to recall that it was a German opera based on a well-known Italian play. Obviously, this was the one. When Lasek realised that his scheme had come to nought, he must simply have abandoned the score and libretto at his lodgings where they were in due course discovered and passed on to me.

'Whilst the music may have been terrible, the play itself was another matter. I knew it to be a famous play, one of Goldoni's best, and the German libretto which had obviously been prepared, judging from the handwriting, by someone other than the composer of the music, seemed to me – and I speak German quite fluently – really very good. All that was needed was a better composer.

'I thought no more about it at the time, but some while later an idea came to me: why not write my own opera based on Goldoni's play using the same German libretto? It was an ambitious idea, but what had I to lose? If it was a success, my fortune would be made.

'I had brought with me from Prague a large quantity of paper to use for musical composition. I had planned, in my airy optimistic mood, to compose a piano concerto and a symphony or two on the long journey to England so that I would have something ready with which to impress the English public, but I am ashamed to say that I did not manage to write a single note before my arrival – not even the merest demisemiquaver.

'The sight of all that virgin paper fair near put me off, I can tell you. I felt like a young sailor about to embark on his maiden voyage looking out over the vast expanse of empty ocean and wondering how his little ship could ever reach the other side.

Nevertheless, I steeled myself to the task of writing my opera

'In truth, I tell you, I had never known anything like it. I know not how or whence the inspiration came but superb arias, duets and choruses poured from my pen in glorious profusion, and the orchestration was beyond the power of words to describe. I wrote it down with hardly an alteration. My score was absolutely original, entirely my own, though sometimes as I worked on it, I sensed Mozart's spirit come upon me as if to encourage me in my endeavours. Yes, it was worthy, worthy even of Mozart himself. It was sublime! Pardon me for my lack of modesty, but, before God, I tell you, Monsieur President, that I, Antoine Vascal, or Antonin Vasylicek as I was then known, composed in London a masterpiece, without doubt a true masterpiece!

'I had only recently finished it when circumstances forced me to leave England, and by a terrible misfortune in my haste to depart I carelessly took with me the wretched score found in Prague and left behind my own – and the libretto too. I only realised my mistake when I had already crossed the sea. There was no going back, not then, not ever.

'After arriving in Paris sometime later, I thought I would be able to reconstruct the score from memory, but I simply couldn't remember a single bar of the music, not one, and the inspiration that I once possessed had entirely deserted me. There was nothing I could do."

"But, Antoine, why have you never told us of this before now?"

'Well, you know me, Monsieur President, I've never been one for sorry tales. Moping and misery are not my style. Besides, I could not bear to think of my opera, my one and only masterpiece, the only worthwhile thing I've ever achieved in my life, carelessly abandoned in a foreign city. I don't suppose…' Antoine continued with a catch in his voice, a small tear coursing gently down his lined old face, 'I don't suppose that it will ever now be performed.

It is lost forever."

An uncharacteristic silence fell upon the assembled throng. There was not a dry eye that evening at the Café Racine as Antoine recounted his sad story.

Everybody knew Antoine as an amiable old charmer, a begetter of pretty musical bagatelles, certainly no genius. On the other hand, nobody for one moment doubted that he had indeed composed a masterpiece. The President declared the proposition to be false. The debate was at an end.

Friday 30th June 2006

The lights dimmed. The low hubbub of chatter in the auditorium quickly petered out. The conductor raised his baton. The world premiere performance of the opera The Servant of Two Masters, attributed to W.A. Mozart, was about to begin at the Royal Opera House, Covent Garden.

All those responsible at the opera house were to be congratulated on a magnificent job in managing to mount a performance of the opera in the short space of time available.

A young, relatively unknown English composer had been commissioned to edit the score and complete the missing parts of it for the purposes of producing a performing edition. For a man whose own compositions generally sounded not unlike a procession of milk floats rattling along a bumpy road before colliding with a brick wall, he had actually made quite a respectable job of preparing the opera for performance, and even the music he wrote to fill in the few gaps in the score sounded almost Mozartian.

A glittering array of the world's most talented soloists had been assembled for the occasion and they were to be accompanied by the orchestra and chorus of the Royal Opera House itself, under the baton of none other than the charismatic Marcus Lismore as guest conductor.

Being one of the most prestigious events to be organised to celebrate the 250th anniversary of Mozart's birth, it was billed as a black-tie gala evening. Within a few days of their release all the tickets – those which had not already been allocated to corporate sponsors – were sold out. Apart from celebrity guests and corporate parties, the audience comprised, with a few exceptions, all the usual sort of people who foregather on such occasions: the Great and the Good, the Wealthy and the Worthy, the Smart, the Smooth and the Smug. It was ever thus.

Justin Wetherby had naturally received a knighthood in the New Year's Honours List for services to music. Flanked by his adoring wife, Sir Justin sat triumphantly alongside the directors and trustees of the Royal Opera House and their respective wives, beaming in a graceful manner to all and sundry. The occasion marked the climax of a distinguished career, and in a kindly gesture of reconciliation he had even waved to his old academic rival sitting close by, but Doctor Digby churlishly pretended not to notice. Never mind, Wetherby thought, he had won and Digby had lost… and that's what really counted.

Glades Design Partnership, the well-known architectural practice, was represented by their senior partner, Gerald Higginbottom, and his wife. He had eventually capitulated to his partners in their desire to change the firm's name, but had insisted, as the price of his co-operation, that the firm should offer to act as one of the co-sponsors of the opera. A not inconsiderable sum was involved.

Without his discovery of the manuscript, Gerald boasted, this splendid gala event would not be taking place, and the Great and the Good would have been denied the opportunity of showing off their cultural credentials, and their wives denied the excuse of visiting Bond Street to kit themselves out for the occasion.

Archie Kendall was there too with his friend Lillian as guests of a Japanese investment bank. Visits to Covent Garden always revived memories of his old friend Hugo, who, but for his tragic death, would surely have been there to provide a witty review of the evening's proceedings.

Poor Archie missed Hugo a great deal. He took Lillian quite often to Chez Véronique for old times' sake, but it simply wasn't the same without Hugo. Lillian was a fine woman and Archie was really very fond of her, but she did take life most awfully seriously. She was so terribly enthusiastic about everything, from her work at the office to art and high culture, from saving the planet to personal health and fitness, from rescuing stray dogs to preserving the habitat of the European spadefoot toad and other species of creature under threat of extinction… virtually everything, in fact, except for sex, of which to date Archie had had none at all, only the occasional modest peck on the cheek. Hugo would have known how to handle this problem, he thought. How he wished he was here now when his advice was so sorely needed.

Dulcie and Dora had managed to obtain some spare tickets at the last moment through a friend of Dulcie's who was married to someone in the orchestra. Dulcie always seemed to know someone useful like that. On Hugo's death, his old Earls Court flat where Dulcie and Dora still lived had passed to his younger brother George, who was a wine merchant by trade. He was quite prepared to allow Dulcie and Dora to remain indefinitely at the flat as his tenants. A likeable, good-looking young man, he too personally collected the rent and came for tea once a month, though his personal revelations were not quite in the same league as those of his older sibling. Dulcie missed Hugo's visits more than she cared to admit.

Frank Belcanto sat, rather glum-faced, with his young lady

friend, Suzie. His company's PR advisors, Louther & Tomkins – the firm by which Lisa was employed – had recommended that it would greatly enhance the company's image if it would agree to become one of the opera's corporate sponsors. Frank, as Chairman and Chief Executive, could scarcely absent himself on such an important occasion. Along with his business guests, a few seats were reserved for friends and family. His cousin Toni was there with his wife, along with Lisa and her new fiancée, Toni's son Joe. The men seemed rather bored by the whole affair, but the girls positively revelled in the glitz and glamour of the evening; not least Suzie, who caused a minor sensation on her arrival by wearing a most sexy, tight-fitting outfit of the kind she used to wear as a nightclub hostess. There was, of course, much tut-tutting from respectable matrons in adjoining rows and not a few sly, envious glances from men when they thought their wives weren't looking.

Mercifully seated in a different part of the auditorium from Frank and his party, Gina was flirting with her new man, a flashy Brazilian playboy with apartments in Rio, London and Paris, a country house in Ireland complete with racing stables, a private jet and a large vulgar motor cruiser moored in the harbour at Portofino.

Old Ted Meadowfield, the senior partner of Messrs Fletcher, Pugh & Meadowfield, heaved a sigh of relief as the lights dimmed. He had glimpsed one of his best clients in the foyer, and he didn't want to be seen that evening by anyone who knew him – not if he could avoid it. The reason was that he was accompanied not by his dear wife Marjorie but by Katie, she of the most engaging smile and shapely thighs, the young trainee solicitor who had first found Eleanor Foxley's diary and posed for such a delightful picture in the local newspaper. Ted and Katie were sharing a luxury suite at a smart boutique hotel in Knightsbridge, while the unfortunate Mrs. Meadowfield had been under the impression that Ted was away in Torquay attending a Law Society conference. By chance she met one of the partners in her husband's firm in the street who, in an unguarded moment, told her that he was unaware of any Law Society conference that weekend in Torquay or elsewhere. It was lucky for Ted that his mobile was switched off and that he rarely got round to checking his messages.

Meanwhile, waiting in the wings, as the orchestra played the short but tuneful overture, there stood, pale-faced and nervous, a pretty young soprano. Sandra Grisewood was about to make her debut performance that evening in the role of the maid Smeraldina. The big moment for which she had waited for so long was about to arrive.

Adam, Sandra's fiancé, hardly able to contain his excitement, sat with his parents, Sir Arthur and Lady Cathcart. Next to them, in the same row, were Albert Grisewood and his wife June and a very proud Gordon Peabody, Sandra's first music teacher.

As Sandra made her appearance on stage, Sir Arthur Cathcart leant over to address the Grisewoods in a hoarse whisper.

"You must be very proud of your daughter."

"Oh yes, we are, Sir Arthur, believe me," Albert Grisewood said, "but of course we always knew Sandra would go far, didn't we, June?" June nodded and smiled. It was quite the happiest moment of her life.

Though the evening was a sell-out, there were inevitably a few empty seats – people who failed to show up due to some last-minute problem: sudden illness, transport delays, business meetings overrunning and so forth. There were two such vacant seats at the end of the back row of the stalls. At least they appeared to be vacant, but they were in fact occupied – if occupied is quite the appropriate word – by phantoms, the phantoms of Hugo Belcher and Antoine Vascal.

As the curtain fell for the last time after many rounds of

applause, Hugo turned to Antoine.

"Well, Antoine, how did you enjoy your opera?"

"There are no words, Hugo, which can adequately convey my delight," Antoine replied in a voice quivering with emotion. "You see, I thought my opera was lost forever. I never thought to hear it actually performed… and it was such a wonderful performance. The conductor, the orchestra, the singers – they were all magnificent!"

"Yes, the performance was quite exceptional, but the star of the show was the music itself, your music. I congratulate you, Antoine. Your opera is a masterpiece! It's just such a shame that you don't get the due credit for it."

"Hugo, the fact that people really believe that my opera was composed by Mozart is reward enough for me."

"Nonetheless, I feel sure that one day somehow the truth will be told, and you will get the credit and recognition you deserve."

"Perhaps, Hugo, perhaps… but now it is time for us to leave."

The pair of them floated silently, as phantoms do, through the dense throng of people shuffling their way towards the exits. Some of the ladies experienced a sudden, oddly cold sensation as Hugo's ghostly hand squeezed a pert breast or patted a shapely bottom as he floated by.

Their progress was much quicker than that of everyone else, of course, and soon they were outside and away, leaving the Royal Opera House far behind them as they floated freely upwards through the night air to rejoin that other world of spirits to which they both belonged.

Epilogue

Monday 14th April, 2025

Bloody Monday again! Duncan Leadbetter moaned to himself as he opened up his shop and went inside, stooping to pick up the post from the mat.

The business was a second-hand bookshop which Duncan had inherited from his father some twenty years or more before. He liked to call himself an antiquarian bookseller. It sounded so much better when people asked him what he did at drinks parties, but, although he did have some old and valuable books which he kept in a locked bookcase at the back of the shop, the stock nowadays comprised books of every age and description.

Duncan hated Mondays. There were generally very few customers and it was boring with only himself for company. The worst thing about Monday, though, was that being such a quiet day, there was no excuse to put off attending to the tedious routine chores for which there might not be time later in the week.

The first thing he always did after looking through the post was to tidy up the shelves. There were always a few gaps left by last week's sales, but the main problem was those bloody customers who came in on Saturdays just to browse. They took books down to look at and then put them back in the wrong place and left without buying anything. Very irritating!

Eventually he came to the section of shelving where the foreign language books were kept. A large tome had fallen on its side, toppling over several other books alongside it.

The fallen volume was called *Le Boulevardier Romantique* by someone called Victor Chavigny and appeared to be his memoirs. Why did I ever buy this book? he moaned. It had been there for longer than he could remember, and no one had ever shown the slightest interest in it.

Mainly as an excuse to delay going on with tidying the shelves, he took the book over to the counter to take a better look at it. Then it came back to him: he had acquired it not long after he had inherited the business, all those years ago, as part of a large collection of books belonging to some deceased person's estate. It was a good collection, well worth the money, and the rest of the books had sold really well – all except for this one. Well, who, after all, would want to buy a book of memoirs in French of some completely unknown dead Frenchman?

On a whim, he flipped through the pages at random and by coincidence alighted upon the first page of a chapter entitled 'La Societé Racine'. Duncan's French was not quite as good as he liked to believe it was. He got the general gist of it, however.

This bloke Chavigny, whoever he was, had gone to meet these other blokes at a café called the Café Racine in Montmartre. They were all members of this society called the Societé Racine, named presumably, like the café, after the famous French dramatist. They were there for a meal and a débat. Presumably, then, the society was a debating society of some kind.

The next bit threw him, though. He had to consult his French dictionary to discover that the word 'genie' in the text didn't only refer to the sort of genie that popped out of Aladdin's lamp, but also meant 'genius', and that 'chef-d'œuvre' didn't mean the bloke in a restaurant whose responsibility it was to prepare the hors d'oeuvre but actually meant a 'masterpiece'.

Of course! He'd got it now. All these earnest chaps were assembled at this café in Montmartre to debate whether or not you had to be a genius to create a masterpiece. Well, really! How very Gallic of them!

If only Duncan had read on a little further, he would have

come upon an account of a fellow called Antoine Vascal and how he had composed in England an opera called The Servant of Two Masters, which he thought was a masterpiece, but then had unfortunately left the score behind when, in haste, he had left his lodgings in London, never to return!

But enough was enough! He returned to the title page: it was a first edition published in Paris in the nineteenth century, in good condition and very well bound. Perhaps it was more valuable than Duncan had given it credit for. Maybe it would appeal to some specialist collector, and perhaps, therefore, it should really be kept in the locked bookcase at the back of the shop, where the serious buyers tended to look. Or perhaps he should advertise it on the internet. He had a website, after all – ought he make use of it?

Eventually, whatever he did, Duncan reassured himself, someone would one day buy this wretched book; someone always did. And, unbeknown to Duncan, that someone, or some later reader, might perhaps reveal to the world the true secret of the Bloomsbury opera.

Notes

As noted this book is a work of fiction, but it is true that Mozart had at least begun to write an opera based on Goldoni's play as evidenced by the letter to his father referred to in the Introduction and elsewhere in the book. All the evidence indicates that Mozart abandoned the opera but that he did write some arias intended for inclusion in it which survive today as separate concert arias. The discovery of an opera score in Bloomsbury based on Goldoni's play is of course a product of the author's imagination.

Carlo Goldoni was born in Venice in 1707 and died in Paris in 1793. Though trained as a lawyer, his interests always inclined towards the theatre. He wrote tragic plays, but soon realised that comedy was his true métier. While it is true that he continued to employ conventional Commedia dell' Arte themes and traditions in his plays, he transformed Italian comedy by making the characters and plots truer to life. No longer are the characters presented as simple stereotypes in the old Commedia dell' Arte tradition. Goldoni wrote more than 150 comedies, of which The Servant of Two Masters is one of the best known and most regularly performed. It was first staged in 1745.

The Vauxhall Pleasure Gardens were originally called New Spring Gardens. They opened around 1661 and closed in 1859. In the late seventeenth century, they became a rather insalubrious place frequented by thieves and prostitutes, but in the first part of 18th century the gardens were transformed under new ownership, and became a popular venue for fashionable society with many attractions, including a cascade, a music room and a Chinese pavilion. From 1792, the charge for admission was the not inconsiderable sum for the time of two shillings.

The gardens, as noted by Antonin, were indeed the site of a rehearsal of Handel's Music for the Royal Fireworks. The rehearsal was attended by a crowd of some 12,000 people and traffic blocked London Bridge for three hours. The first formal performance, which took place in Green Park on 27th April 1749, was, if the pun may be forgiven, a bit of a damp squib. It was a rainy evening and one of the buildings, purpose-built for the occasion, caught fire. Everyone, though, would undoubtedly have enjoyed the music!

Joseph Haydn (1732–1809) was born in the village of Rohrau in lower Austria, the son of a wheelwright. In his early life, he became a choirboy at St Stephen's Cathedral in Vienna, and most of his adult career was spent in the service of the Esterházy family as Kapellmeister (composing, playing and directing music) at the Palace of Esterházy. When Prince Nikolaus Esterházy died in 1790, Haydn became free to travel, and, at the invitation of the musical impresario Saloman, he came to London in 1791, the first of two visits, the second commencing in 1794. It was during his time in London that Haydn composed the twelve famous London Symphonies including The Surprise, The Miracle (referred to below), The Military, The Clock, The Drum Roll and The London. Haydn is renowned for his symphonies, string quartets, his oratorios The Creation and The Seasons, and his great settings of the Mass. He did, however, also write a good many operas, which in recent years have rightly become more highly regarded. Several were based on libretti by Goldoni, of which Il Mondo della Luna (the World of the Moon) is probably the best known. His German opera for marionettes, Philemon und Baucis, was first performed at Esterházy in September 1773 in the new marionette theatre in the presence of the Empress Maria Theresa. Uncle Jan refers to an incident when a chandelier nearly fell on him after a performance of a Haydn symphony. This refers to an occasion in February

1795 when a huge chandelier fell down onto an area of seating just vacated by the audience. The symphony concerned became known as The Miracle, the miracle being that no one was injured. For many years, this title was erroneously given to Symphony number 96, but the incident actually occurred after the first performance of the B flat Symphony number 102.

Baldassarre Galuppi (1706–1785) came from the island of Burano in the Venetian lagoon and was nicknamed Il Buranello. He was a gifted composer, and like Goldoni, had a talent for mixing and contrasting the farcical with the serious, the better to produce dramatic and comic effects of a more interesting and varied nature. It would be fair to describe Galuppi as a pivotal figure in the development of the comic opera genre, which would later culminate in the great comic masterpieces of Mozart and Rossini. The taste for musical theatre was strong in Italy during the eighteenth century, hence Goldoni's association with Galuppi for whom he provided the libretti for several operas, though not, so far as is known, one for The Servant of Two Masters. No score of such an opera was ever in fact found in the monastery library at San Martino di Roccabella, for the very simple reason that Father Gesualdo and all the other holy monks, indeed the very Abbey itself and the town of Roccabella (as well as the erudite Professor Tolentini), are all figments of the author's imagination. An opera based on The Servant of Two Masters was, though, composed by the twentieth-century Italian-American composer Vittorio Giannini to a libretto by Bernard Stambler.

Prince Dimitri Mikhailovich Galitzin was the Russian Ambassador in Vienna for thirty years from 1762. He became one of Mozart's greatest friends and patrons after Mozart moved to Vienna from Salzburg.

Since Eleanor Foxley (like Professors Wetherby and Tolentini, Victor Chavigny, the Cathcart family the rogue Lasek and others) is another figment of the author's imagination, there was no such meeting with Haydn at Esterházy, as described in this book. Whether Prince Galitzin was aware of Mozart's intention to write an opera based on Goldoni's play and could have enlightened us as to whether it was ever completed or not, we therefore do not know. Nor do we know whether Haydn ever contemplated composing an opera based on the same play. One suspects, though, that if Haydn was familiar with the play, he would have found it as appealing a potential opera plot as Mozart evidently did.

The puppet play with incidental music by Haydn L'Assedio di Gibilterra was indeed performed at the marionette theatre at Esterházy as described in Eleanor Foxley's diary on the 20th August 1783 during 'Eleanor's visit'.

The composer **Gioacchino Rossini** (1792–1868) was also a great lover of food and wine. The famous dish known as Tournedos Rossini is thought to have been dedicated to Rossini by the chef at the Maison Dorée in Paris. Several other dishes were also named after him.

Rossini spent several years of his life in Paris and had regular tables at several restaurants there, including Bofinger, Maison Dorée and La Tour d'Argent, though whether he repaired to the Maison Dorée after the performance of Le Comte Ory, as postulated in this book, the author has no idea. Le Comte Ory is a splendid French comic opera in which the rakish Comte Ory endeavours to seduce a countess, gaining access to her castle disguised as a nun. It was premiered at the Académie Royale de Musique on the 20th August 1828.

Josef Mysliveček (1737–1781), whom Antonin mentions in the episode at 'the Café Racine', was born in Prague, the son (one of twins) of a wealthy Prague miller. From 1763 onwards, although he continued regularly to visit Prague, Vienna and Munich, he settled permanently in Italy, where he was known as Il Boemo (the Bohemian). He wrote operas, oratorios, concertos, a great many symphonies and much chamber music. Mozart himself had a high regard for Mysliveček, who is sometimes also referred to as 'the Czech Mozart'.

This book hardly gives due credit to the professional and painstaking way in which musicologists go about their business. However, misattributions of musical works obviously do occasionally occur, in the same way that art experts have sometimes falsely attributed paintings to the wrong artist. A striking example is the symphony for a long time attributed to Mozart (as his symphony No.37, K.444) but which later was realised to have been composed by Michael Haydn, Joseph's younger brother. The confusion may have arisen because Mozart did actually write a twenty-bar slow introduction to the first movement. As with many prolific composers, there is a long list of works by Mozart, the scores of which have been lost. Many, though not all, are works from Mozart's early life. Amongst many examples is a Trumpet Concerto, referred to in a letter to his father dated 12th November 1768. How one would dearly love to hear that!

So far as concerns works later in Mozart's career, there may be a missing minuet from the famous serenade Eine kleine Nachtmusik K.525. According to Mozart's own catalogue, the serenade has five movements, rather than the four which we know today.

And new discoveries do from time to time occur. For example, the score of Haydn's puppet opera Philemon und Baucis, already referred to, was believed lost in the great fire at Esterházy in 1779 along with the scores of his other marionette operas, but it turned up in a Paris saleroom in 1965. Another good example was the rediscovery of Haydn's C major cello concerto in 1961, a concerto which has been regularly performed and recorded ever since. A magnificent setting of the Dixit Dominus was recently discovered to be by Vivaldi, formerly falsely attributed to Galuppi.

In 1996 the manuscript score of an opera called Der Stein der Weisen (The Philosopher's Stone) kept in the Hamburg City Theatre collection was found to contain Mozart's name over several of the musical numbers. The work was composed at the instigation of Emanuel Schikaneder (the actor and impresario who worked with Mozart on The Magic Flute), and was apparently a collaborative effort on the part of four composers including Mozart, so only some of it (less than twenty minutes in fact) was by Mozart himself. Nevertheless, this was obviously a fascinating discovery.

In September 2008, a musical score on a single, small scrap of paper was found in a library in Nantes in France. The score is in Mozart's own hand and appears to be part of a previously unknown setting of a Credo in D Major, as well as the draft of a second piece which is mostly illegible – clearly a most important new find. Perhaps, on some dusty library shelf or dark corner of an attic in Prague, Paris, Vienna or London there lurks, awaiting discovery, the score of Mozart's German opera Der Diener Zweier Herren. Who knows?

About the author

Tim Davidson lives in Bristol and is a retired lawyer. He is married with two grown-up children, Thomas and Nicholas. His wife, Maddalena, is Italian, from the Veneto region of northern Italy, and a teacher by profession. Tim has had a life-long passion for classical music and opera.